Stricken

Book 5 in the Jones Star Series

By

Marlene Bierworth

Copyright © 2018 Marlene Bierworth

All rights reserved.

No part of this book may be reproduced by any means, graphic, electronic, or mechanical including photocopying, recording, taping or by any information storage retrieval system without written permission of the author, Marlene Bierworth, except in the case of brief quotations embodied in critical articles and reviews.

Disclaimer

This book is a work of fiction. Names, places, character and events are the product of the author's imagination. While the author has tried to be historically correct, her goals in this book are great characters and storytelling. Any resemblance to actual persons, living or dead, events or locals, is purely coincidental.

From the Author

Welcome to Book 5 in the Jones Star Series. Although this story is complete in itself, the characters and family subplots flow from book to book to create the new adventure.

Take a peek at the entire series here:

https://www.amazon.com/author/marlenebierworth

It is my purpose to provide a sweet western romance set in the frontier days, full of adventure, love, hardships, defeats and victories of the fictitious Jones family. The content is light on history and heavy on character, dreams and storytelling. It is faith based, which is the epiphany of love and my personal happy-ever-after.

The book **Stricken** features Clare Jones, and depicts her story of finding love in this new land. The drama unfolds in the latter 1800's in Montana territory. The series continues as a family saga: Life and love for the Jones' in Aspen Glen. I hope you will enjoy this new adventure with the ever expanding Jones family and friends.

Stricken is a story of a second chance at love, rebuilding destroyed dreams, and the joy of discovering that God has a plan for Clare Jones. Love becomes an emotional battle, hindered by past hurts and two very different men pursuing her in the present.

Love – is it worth fighting for? You bet it is!

Come join the fans at **Romance: The Jones-Star Family,** FB group to interact

https://www.facebook.com/groups/1118008614903688/

See all this author's titles on **Amazon Author Page**

https://www.amazon.com/-/e/B00J9RM116

Sign up for my newsletter and receive a weekly inspiration and book deals.

http://eepurl.com/djNqjn

Chapter 1

With my hands caked in powdery flour, I crept up behind the unsuspecting man. Lively intentions itched at my fingers to create chaos in my kitchen with a man I barely knew. This was so unlike me. The mere idea of spontaneous fun had long since gone by the wayside – especially all possibilities that included men. A slow-dying marriage will do that to you. I couldn't recall a time when I felt so full of life in the presence of a man. Somehow, this wake-up call didn't fill me with my well-acquainted fear or quench the spirited scheme bubbling inside me, but instead spurred me forward. I dared to imagine that perhaps it was Drake, my son's hired cook, who had the power to awaken the emotions held captive inside me for too many years.

I grinned at the seriousness of the man. Surely I'd missed-the-mark entirely! No one would ever suspect Drake could stir anything in anyone at this particular moment. His directed stare concentrated solely on the sugary scum building atop the boiling berries. By all indications, the man had forgotten I was even in the room.

Temptation won out. It was a pleasant day for fun and we

both could use a break from canning. Standing on my tiptoes, I poked my head around to face his and landed a thick smear of white powder down his willowy nose. He startled and jumped back. I tumbled, but not before I witnessed a cloud of confusion cover his features and then his eyes lighting up with the response I'd hoped for.

"What do we have here? A challenge to a flour fight, in this kitchen that we will have to clean up afterward?" he asked.

"You think too much," I said as I dove forward and ran my hands down both tanned cheeks then scurried to the side to avoid his flailing reach in my direction.

"You have an unfair advantage. I never saw this coming or I'd been prepared," he said.

"I passed him some leftover ammunition sitting in the bottom of a mixing bowl. "Defend yourself. I plan on winning."

The next few minutes found the contents of the dish emptied over the floor and us, and even as I considered the additional work compounded onto an already hot and busy day, I never retreated. I desired more than anything, to do something silly, and in watching his reaction, figured Drake did as well. We landed on the floor with a thump and I rolled over on my back, overcome with side-splitting hysterics. He untangled his long legs and arms from mine then stretched out his solid frame beside me. He exhaled deeply. Spinning to his side, he propped his head on his elbow and beamed like a young boy.

"I think I won this battle, my lady," he said while rifling his fingers through his wavy graying hair. He tossed his head back and laughed. "Woman, you are making a wreck of me."

"I surrender. You are stronger and move like a flash of lightning." I garbled the words, but the tease came across unmistakably clear.

He jumped to his feet. Somehow those lanky legs did his bidding with ease. I could only wish that my energy and strength would respond so quickly. Drake reached for my hand, pulled me up and dropped me onto a nearby kitchen chair – just in time to see the pot boil over. We both reacted. Bounding forward, we tripped over one another unable to stop the merriment from sifting into the chaotic situation. Bent over in laughter, we both giggled and moaned our way to the cook stove.

"Now look what you've gone and done," Drake said.

"Seems to me that batch was your responsibility," I tossed the blame back on him. As we both moved the pot off the black top and grabbed for scrub cloths. "You realize this is going to be a nasty clean up? Not to mention a waste of preserves for the men at the camp dining hall."

"I'm thinkin' this here pot of jam was targeted for the Jones' kitchen. Has a nice burnt aroma that PJ will surely love."

"PJ is your boss. You best behave," I warned.

We'd passed beyond the point of no return, for now we found ourselves chuckling at nonsense. We interpreted everything as funny. It appeared when I let the dam loose inside I couldn't stop the overflow. But, our cheerfulness was cut short by the signaling of someone clearing his throat.

"Sorry to barge in on your fun Clare, but with all the noise coming from inside this room you never heard me knocking. I let myself in." I was hoping to see a smile on Robert's face, but instead, his expression of confusion and annoyance said it all.

"You will be happy to note, Doctor Palatsie, that both of us have avoided any burns or damage to our bodies. Saved you a house call – but then again, here you are calling on us anyway."

I tried to refrain from giggling at my words. *Get a grip*! I summoned up my serious face.

"Is this an official call?" I asked.

Panic shifted me into desperate mode as I thought of my family so far off in Boston.

"Have you heard news from Patrick? Are they well?"

"There's no news from your son, Clare."

Looking at his stern face, I suddenly felt reprimanded, like a child. Robert was a no-nonsense type, stable and self-assured – all the qualities a woman needed to feel safe. I supposed my cutting-loose with Drake appeared rather foolish to an onlooker. But the joy lingered and I could not entirely scold myself for the lark that we'd just shared. Robert's expression never flinched but remained sober and impatient.

Drake broke the awkward silence. "Sorry for the mess, Doc. Would ya like a cup-of-Joe?"

"No time. I'm in a hurry." His tone dismissed Drake. Robert attempted to hide the glare as his eyes focused on me. "Clare, I came to ask if you'd consider accompanying me to the next valley. Lots of sick folks to care for and I could use a hand."

"Me? I'm not a nurse, Robert," I said.

"You're a mother who has healed lots of fevers and sat at bedsides and prayed. You can follow instructions, right? That's all I need." His manner took on the form of begging.

Drake butted in. "What kind of sickness? Surely not the plague. Ya wouldn't be bringin' her into a scene like that, would ya, Doc?" I sensed the concern in Drake's voice and placed my hand on his arm. The doctor responded to his question with a shrug.

"There are people who need our help, Drake. What kind of a Christian would I be if I did not respond with compassion?" I moved closer to where Robert stood. "When are you leaving?"

"As soon as you can be ready. I have my bags packed and waiting in the buggy. I'll send word to Stanley if I need additional supplies." He was all business and I sensed his urgency.

I glanced at Drake.

"I'm sorry to leave you with such a mess." I couldn't hide the hint of a smile after that statement, but Drake's mood had unexpectedly turned to ice.

"One you instigated, I might add," Drake said as he headed to the stove. He mumbled under his breath, as equally somber as the doctor now. "He comes a callin' and off she goes, nary a thought fer her safety. Crazy woman."

"Drake you are mumbling a pile of nonsense. Surely you can see the doctor needs help with this medical crisis," I said.

He turned on his heels to face us. "I can see he needs help, but why you?" He avoided making eye contact with me. I was dumbfounded. This was so unlike Drake, or at least the man I'd grown to know. We'd been harvesting, cooking and preserving together for weeks, both of us eager to feed the men and Jones family this coming winter. It had been fun to share my kitchen with someone else while Patrick and Ruth Ellen were in Boston. Isolation had plagued me while living alone in the big house, so the hours spent with Drake had helped to fill the long days.

"I am honored that the doctor felt confident to ask me. I don't understand your hesitation, Drake." *Or your right to create such a scene*, I might have added but did not.

He hesitated. At length, his words spluttered out. "Lots of preserving left to do."

"Silly man. We can pick up when I get back." I touched his shoulder gently, not wanting to leave on hostile terms. "In your heart, I know you don't believe that food takes precedence over people's lives. Please, tell PJ when he returns where I am and that I am being careful."

"Yes, and tell her son that I'll watch out for her as well," Robert said emphasizing her son, noticeably not caring what the cook thought. "No harm will come her way."

"You can't guarantee that, Doc," Drake said. "Sickness is like a serpent rattlin' in the tall grass not carin' who it strikes."

I was touched by the concern etched in Drake's face. He attempted to cover it with his back-to-business expression and slipped back into his place of comfort.

"I'll clean up here and close the door behind me. Be goin' back to the mess hall where I belong."

I wondered what that comment implied, but this was not the time to question Drake further. He'd tuned me out and busied himself with the task at hand. The room was strained, and without even looking, I felt Robert's impatience. I turned toward him.

"I'll try to hurry, Robert. Please help yourself to coffee while I go pack a bag and clean up."

I could hear clearly the age-old advise from my deceased mother echo in my ear – *silliness after forty is not becoming of a lady*. And to top it off, the sensible Doctor had caught Drake and me in our folly. It's a wonder that he'd followed through in asking for my help with such a serious health situation.

"Thank you, Clare. I'd appreciate that. Last I heard the sick are all being transferred into one building that they use for all sorts of town events. It'll make our job easier having them all together. It's fast becoming an epidemic."

As I sped up the stairs, my mind wandered back to the kitchen scene and I wondered how long the doctor had been standing in the kitchen doorway before he spoke, and how much he'd seen of my carrying on with another man. Not that we were officially courting, but I knew that the family was encouraging us in that direction. *Robert was a respectable man and would make a trustworthy caring husband*. My son had assured me many times of this fact, attempting to squelch my fears of stepping into another marriage after disaster number one. But, the question of what I wanted for my future remained? Most times, the answer was simple – nothing! I was content to continue my life exactly as things were now.

Upstairs the wash-up took longer than I'd hoped. White flour dust had settled into the strands of my dark trusses and combing through it was laborious. I quickly wound it into a knot at the back of my head and fastened it securely with pins. After managing to stumble into a fresh but simple cotton dress, I sighed when at last I stood redressed – in the middle of the day. How absurd! I'd fumbled at every task and I blamed my jitters on the two men who waited downstairs for my return. I threw random garments into my floral-patterned travel case and jammed the lid shut. In the hallway I paused. The full-length mirror revealed a middle-aged woman of modest appearance. It suited my mission and provided me the confidence I needed to embark upon my next frontier adventure. Clutching my bag tighter, I rebuked my vanity and hurried toward the stairs.

Two hours later, Robert steered the team down the main street of Stanton, a small settlement in the next valley that time and progress forgot. The buildings were covered with plain boards, unpainted with gaping holes showing movement inside. There appeared to be no town pride here, not like the more prosperous Aspen Glen, and the few people that strolled on the dirt road wore heavy expressions. All things considered, the population was suffering an epidemic of sickness, and I should be kinder in my evaluation of their homes and businesses. Robert directed the horses to the far end of town where a small solitary building perched. It was in poor repair, and my heart already broke for the patients waiting inside for a touch of hope from the good doctor.

And me, I reminded myself. Again, I pondered why Robert had sought my help in this crisis. I realized the man did not employ a nurse, and even as a relative newcomer to Aspen Glen, I could see that the population in his rather enormous territory grew greater in size every day.

In the end, the belief that I could be put to good use as God's hand extended, settled the nerves swirling at will inside me. I determined not to fail the Lord – or Doctor Palatsie – who for whatever reason had placed his trust in me. I could easily follow instructions and perhaps even perform the minor tasks of a nurse. Mostly I desired to offer the many infected patients encouragement and a tiny measure of faith.

All these thoughts ran through my mind as the buggy drew near the site of the makeshift hospital. Wagons continued to pull into the area from all directions, stopping and unloading their sick. Men, women, and children, wrapped in blankets like mummies, brought to mind carcasses prepared for burial. I gulped and nearly choked at the bleak, helpless picture these families presented. I glanced at the doctor and noted his concern.

"They should have called for me sooner," he said. A man rushed toward our buggy as Robert pulled on the brake.

"Doc, yer a sight fer sore eyes. The room's nearly full. Not lookin' good at all."

"Tom, good to see you standing on your own two feet. The sickness here appears far worse than your wire suggested," said Robert.

"They just keep comin'. A couple of ladies are doin' the rounds placing cool cloths on foreheads. We had to tie a few down to keep them from running outside stark naked. Fever makin' them all crazy-like. No one knows what to do."

"Well, I'm here now," said the doctor. "Can you carry in the crates I brought?"

"I'm here to do yer biddin', Doc – yours and the lovely lady," said Tom. "Jes call and I'll come a runnin'."

As we entered the cloakroom, the doctor motioned to a corner to the left of the door. "Tom, put the supplies over there. Can you drag over a table and I'll use the space for the main station?"

I wandered into the adjoining room ahead of Robert and stopped in my tracks. I covered my mouth and nose with my hands and swayed. Robert's hand stroked my back and ran the full length of my spine. His intimate touch startled me.

"Are you going to be alright?" he asked.

"The smell is ghastly! Sickness will thrive in this environment. Surely no one will recover."

Robert spoke close to my ear while his eyes scanned the room. "Why don't you go and open the windows. If you have trouble grab a strong arm to help you. It's August and hot. A draft is the last thing these patients have to worry about." He sighed. "Put your apron on and then catch up to me when you're ready."

I smiled and tried to sound reassuring. "You can count on me, Robert. I won't fall apart on you."

"I have no doubt. Why do you think I chose you as the one to come?"

"To be honest, I don't know."

"You are the most caring person I know, and I desperately needed your help." He cleared his throat. "Besides, you are easy on the eyes, and when mine grow weary, I'll simply glance your way and rejuvenate myself."

I smiled as my hand automatically moved upward to finger a strand of escaped hair and wind it firmly behind my ear. Immediately I dropped my shaky hand, seared by the fire of a shameful flush as it crawled up the back of my neck. "Well, we best get to work then, Doctor. Your patients await."

On my way to the first window, I sidestepped piles of vomit, and by the time the last reluctant pane of glass jiggled open under my persistent tug, I'd jumped over multiple brown puddles of loose diarrhea. The place reeked, and the gentle breeze that worked its way across the room did little to help.

I glanced at the two women who wiped foreheads while holding a hankie to cover their nose, totally ignoring the state of their surroundings. I did not suppress the need to take charge. I marched over to the closest one.

"My name is Clare. I am Doctor Palatsie's assistant." That got her attention. She jumped to her feet, and the hankie slipped revealing a teenage girl.

"My name is Dierdra. I remembered Ma bathing my head in cool water when the fever hit at home. So that's what I'm doing, Ma'am."

"I see that. Thank you. Where is your mother?" I asked.

"She sent me here to care for my sister. She has the sickness. I sorta move around the room when the little one falls asleep."

"Thank you once again. Do you know where to find some sudsy water and a pail? These messes on the floor must be cleaned up."

"Oh Ma'am, that job ain't fer me. I'd upchuck fer sure." The young girl turned a tainted shade of green.

"Perhaps the other woman over there can do it?" I asked.

"She stares out the window at lot. Her man be real sick. One of the first to arrive."

"Well, if you can provide the pail of water and a floor cloth I will do it myself," I said not sure this was the most impressive first job in my new position.

"Yes, Ma'am. I'll be back quick as a jackrabbit."

She hurried off, and I made my way to the corner where Tom had set the supplies down. I rummaged through my bag and drew out a full, heavily starched apron. I pulled the bib top over my head and then tied the straps tightly around my waist. Taking a deep breath, I went to find Robert. He was bent over a patient.

"Robert, I've sent for wash water. There is vile all over the floor that requires cleaning. I'll find you again when I'm done."

"Thank you, Clare. You are a brave woman. Tie a damp hankie over your mouth and nose, and be sure to wash your hands with strong soap when you're done. Until we know the source of this sickness, we're working in the dark here."

"I'll be careful. Don't worry."

The next hour I spent on my knees, and besides cleaning the disgusting puddles the patients left on the floor, I used the time to petition God. It was vital to understand how these people were infected to stop the widespread sickness, and while we waited for the mystery to unfold, I placed my trust in the Lord to send the answer before too many passed from this world. The few faces that I'd witnessed lying beneath the blankets were already ashen, with death's shadow haunting their eyes.

I dumped the soiled water far from the hospital – I decided that's what I'd call the building despite all signs that suggested a more unfavorable title. Giving it a name provided an authentic and viable hope. I hurried back and found a washbasin, filled it with warm water from a pot simmering on the stove for medical purposes, then searched in a box to find a bar of soap. I scrubbed my hands, palms, tops, and between the fingers, until they were rough and red. That should kill whatever poison lay in the brown puddles that had transferred to me.

A voice called from the other side of the room. "Clare!" I looked to find Robert beckoning me over. "Hurry."

While dodging bodies, I arrived at the doctor's side as quickly as I could. His eyes were sad. "We're going to lose this one, Clare. That's his wife, and she is going berserk on me. Can you tend to her?"

I glanced to the spot he indicated and saw that he referred to the second woman helper that I'd briefly encountered while mopping the floors. She had professed to be *in-the-know* of *all-things-important*, and had claimed the young girl, Deidra, to be useless, accomplishing nothing of value except to cry for her sister and to wipe sweat from foreheads. She on the other hand, had martyred for two long days, leaving her children home to fend for themselves in the daylight, and then working half the night to catch up on family chores. She'd declared all this to me while I slopped the messes that she had conveniently left to rot. Now, instead of Deidra, she was the one shedding the tears as she watched her husband slip into eternity.

"Come and sit with me on the steps," I said. "What's your name, again?"

"My man, Ernie, calls me Bessie but I was baptized, Beth Anne."

"Well then, Beth Anne, why don't you come and dry your tears in the sunlight and tell me about your man."

She took one final look at the gagging patient and raised her head high.

"Not much to tell 'ceptin' he's a no good leach who worked me near to the bone and left me with six children to care fer."

Her blatant honesty caught me by surprise. "But the tears?" I was confused.

"Tis the proper way to mourn fer my young'un's father. I'm not a cold woman."

I wrapped an arm around her stiff shoulders and led her outside, not sure if even she completely understood what kind of woman she was. I most certainly was in doubt. Her red hair was matted and her breath stank sour from something she chewed on. Tobacco? Did women do that in the West? We sat together on the front step of the building, and I sucked in the fresh air to clear my foggy brain.

"Tell me about your children, Beth Anne," I asked.

She began to ramble, and I could sense the pride she had in her *brood* as she called them. The oldest was only eleven years old, and I wondered how on earth she would manage to raise this young family alone.

"How will you make a living? Do you farm or have cattle to sell?" I asked when the curiosity got the better of me.

I was not expecting her brazen reply; then again, I was beginning to expect the unexpected with this woman.

"Got me a few chickens and a milkin' cow. But it don't matter none. I won't be alone fer long." She sat erect and gazed off into the distance.

"Will relatives come to help you, then?" I asked.

"Oh, there be no need for the likes of them! Got me a man waitin' on the sidelines. Been seein' him fer a while now, but we both feared my husband. He'd kill Teddy faster than you could blink an eye. But this here sickness done did the job fer us. Won't be grievin' long, Ma'am. Don't you worry yourself none."

So much for comforting a grieving widow. If all frontier women were this prepared for the death of a spouse, my job might be easier than I suspected.

"Well, if you don't need me anymore, I'll go back and help the doctor. You best return home and prepare for the funeral. I'll be praying for you, Bessie, and your family."

Upon my final evaluation of the woman, Bessie seemed the more appropriate name for this new widow. What on earth had I gotten myself into?

Chapter 2

One of the families, the Wrights, offered to house us in an outside shed-of-sorts located on their small piece of land on the outskirts of town. And although they appreciated all that the doctor and I did for the small community, they feared contamination more and would not permit us within a hundred yards of the main house, let alone inside it. Someone in the family always took note of our comings and goings, for whenever either of us arrived at the small shanty a picnic box of food was delivered and left at the door.

"Chicken legs and salad," a timid voice called out. I watched through the window until the teenager had retreated a safe distance.

Opening the door wide, I waved at the girl who stood guard watching until someone retrieved the bounty of food. "Thank you," I called out.

"Yer welcome. Ma said to ask how it was going at the sick house. Any more dead?"

Her question was so to the point that one might imagine these folks heartless – but I knew better. The people living here, along with the ones that staggered in from beyond the town limits, all cared deeply but kept their distance. Fatalities and violence had struck this part of the country before, and they all believed that the death angel lingered very close by – capable and eager to strike its victims at will. The whole society seemed to hold their breath – as if letting it out would bring attention to their existence and wreak havoc on their well-being.

The girl stood by waiting to hear my answer to her question. I sighed, knowing the report would not bring hope to the hopeless.

"Two dead today and more patients arriving. Until we find the source of the contamination, the sickness will continue. Please urge your men-folk to find a common link so we can end these useless deaths."

A sober man, with holes in his pants and wearing a shirt too tight for comfort, approached his daughter and touched her shoulder. When she looked, he nodded toward the house and she sped away.

"We have eliminated water as the source. I hope that helps some, Mrs. Jones."

"It does, Mr. Wright. At least, we will know we are not feeding the epidemic when we use water in our treatments. The patients are extremely thirsty in this heat. The summer humidity does not want to let up."

"Some of the patients speak about enjoying a harvest feast before taking ill. Perhaps you could investigate a food item they may have in common or something they put in the gardens to fertilize the soil."

"That's a good idea, Ma'am. We'll keep searching. How ya holdin' up? Ya must be bone weary by now."

"It is exhausting, but God is my strength, and I am pleased to be going about his work," I said.

"My family prays fer the Doc and you every day – more

than once," Mr. Wright said.

"And we feel your prayers. Thank you." I picked up the basket of food. "I should eat and lie down for a spell. Doctor Palatsie will need his time away from the hospital soon. He is overtaxed with worry and lack of supplies."

"Heard there was a wagonload headed our way from Livingston," he said.

"Bless them. We'll watch for it."

I waved again and turned to walk inside. After the door closed, I leaned against it and closed my eyes. When I reopened them, the cot that took up the majority of the small space looked very inviting to my fatigued body, but at the same time, I realized that I had to eat to endure this tiresome undertaking. It would do no good for me to get sick as well, yet both Robert and I understood that the contagions could just as easily attack us. We were so close we could smell death, and the young woman, Deidra, who'd chosen to stay after our arrival had already fallen ill.

I never let on to Robert, but I was experiencing the same symptoms of weakness that I'd often experienced while living in Boston. Now, I began to wonder if they had redeveloped from too much activity on my part or merely a depressed state of mind. Perhaps both. This whole valley lay soaked in despair, and the epidemic only made it worse. At times the dark shadow that lurked in every corner moved in to squeeze the very life from me.

I shook the negative thoughts from my mind. Drama had never been my response to the ills of life, and I'd not entertain it today in Stanton.

At a wooden table, which consisted mainly of two short but wide planks sitting atop four shaky, spindly legs, I opened the basket and withdrew a plate of hot food. The smell of fried chicken invaded my senses, and I had to refocus and sit to keep from swaying. I hadn't eaten since last night and my stomach was reacting to this enticing aroma. I bit into the meat and closed my eyes. The woman of the house was a fine cook and I appreciated this family sharing meals from their kitchen. I had no idea if they could afford to feed us, or not. When this was all over, perhaps PJ would offer the Wright family one of his cattle as a thank you for supplying his mother and the doctor with food during the community crisis. I shoveled the mashed potato in behind the meat and munched on a few carrot sticks. Sighing, I repacked the basket, set it outside the door for pick-up, and crawled on top of the lumpy mattress. A gentle breeze from a nearby window brushed across my face and then blissful sleep swept over me.

It was dark when I awoke. I jumped from the bed, scolding myself for sleeping too long. Robert must be exhausted. I splashed some room-temperature water over my face and toweled it dry. Glancing into an old cracked mirror that hung on the wall was a mistake. I sighed and grabbed up a brush, attempting to tame the bedhead hairdo. My dark locks of yesteryear now revealed strands of silver. The invasion was attractive most days, but today it seemed too many had joined the forces of aging me.

"Fickle!" I chided myself. The sick don't care what I look like, but Robert had implied that he appreciated viewing me from time to time. He was a strange sort of man when it came to opening up emotionally. At times it appeared that he harbored feelings for me, but then his tongue would get tangled and his voice choked on the words that stuck midway in his throat. Awkward silences always followed and left me feeling cheated and shut out from discovering the real man that hid within.

I threw down the brush and hurried toward the door. The doctor would not be looking my way tonight. I'd order him back to this shanty as soon as I got to the hospital.

When I stepped inside the door I was met with an odd silence. I grabbed my apron, which had been cleaned and laid to dry by some unknown woman, and rushed into the main room. Robert lounged in a straight-backed chair at the opposite end of the room with his head tilted to one side resting on a cabinet. Even from this distance I could hear his soft snoring. I smiled. Scanning the entire room, it appeared everyone had halted from suffering for this brief moment of time. The silence – although eerie, as if standing on a precipice waiting to step off into the abyss – was a welcome relief from torment of reality.

I touched Robert's hand and when his eyes flew open, I placed a finger across my mouth. He responded to my gentle tug and I led him toward the door.

"It's your turn. You'll twist your neck on that chair and the cot is so much more comfortable."

"You talking about the same cot I sleep in?"

I appreciated his attempt at humor. "Keep the jokes coming, sir. It may be all that saves your sanity before this is over."

He glanced behind him, as if suddenly remembering he had patients to tend to. I continued to haul him outward.

"Miraculously, they are all asleep. Go! I will send someone to waken you should an emergency arise." From day one, men took turns guarding the hospital, every hour of the day, should the caregivers or the gravedigger need their assistance.

"Thank you, Clare, for everything," Robert said. "I don't know what I'd have done without you this past week."

"My pleasure and duty. Now off with you, and be sure to have breakfast before you head back," I said.

"Yes, Ma'am." I watched him go, dragging one foot behind the other in the direction of our mutual retreat.

I sighed and turned back toward the hospital room. With utmost quietness, I inched forward, sitting upon the same chair

chair that Robert had just deserted. I relaxed and soaked in the warmth of his body that still permeated through the wood. I'd like to say the odor of his woodsy aftershave comforted me but its appeal had long since dissipated. It had been many days since the doctor had used his razor. The scruffy beard would probably compliment a younger man, but the bristle only served to drag Robert's face into long, hard angles. I snickered inside. I was a fine one to speak. How I longed for a tub of hot bubbly water to lie in with enough tangy fragrance to cover the stench of sickness and soak off all the tell-tale grime of my stay in Stanton.

I settled in and glanced across the room. It was my turn to take up the watch and pray, until some dear soul called out for any meagre assistance I could offer. Now was not the time to clean or walk about. Rest was the order of the night, and I prayed it would bring an adequate dose of healing for the body, mind and soul to these inflicted patients.

Sometime before daybreak, the groaning began. It seemed after the first one broke he silence the others followed suit. I moved from person to person with a cool cloth to ease the heat of fever and wipe the dripping sweat from reaching their frightened eyes. A child began to flail and I knew the vomit was coming. I grabbed the pail and pushed her to a sitting position where she proceeded to gag and strain until the watery substance turned pink. I groaned. She was so young, with her whole life ahead of her.

"Dear God, spare this child," I whispered. The patient sunk back onto her blanket and coiled into a ball. I pushed the wet strands of tangled hair from her face, then stood and moved on to the next. It was endless pain and grief.

To my right, I heard the stifled scream and saw the woman jump from her sleeping position. She swayed and I caught her before she collapsed onto a nearby patient. Immediately, I recognized her need, and lifted her worn dress over the rim of a pail and balanced her there. At least this was one mess I would not have to clean off the floor. Her bowel movement went from yesterday's mild and watery to todays severe and gut wrenching. She bent over and groaned, and as the pain reached her eyes she gazed at me through a misty veil. I offered a faint smile and hoped she drew encouragement from it. I'd become proficient at balancing pails and people, and now managed to separate the two without any mishaps or spills. She then collapsed into a heap on the floor.

    I rushed to the clean water supply and filled her cup. Relatives had supplied a cup for their patient when they dropped them off at the hospital. Initially, Robert believed it would discourage the spread of further contamination, at least in the drinking compartment, by not sharing the pouring ladle amongst the sick. Even though the water source had been eliminated as a contagion, it would not hurt to continue the practice as a precaution. The sooner more sources could be removed from the investigation, the sooner this nightmare would be over. Daily, the dead were carried out, and before the floor had a chance to cool, newly infected patients took their place. The blankets and clothes of the deceased were burned and the cycle continued until I grew dizzy from the fast turnarounds.

    Now, over two weeks in, I could not hide my weakness any longer. One morning, I turned to do the doctor's bidding, when instead, fell headlong into his arms. When I awoke, I was in the shed with the brave teen from the house hovering outside the door. She called out to me.

    "Ma'am, you okay? Doc says fer me not to dare leave this spot till ya send me away on yer own accord."

    I struggled to a sitting position and grabbed for a glass of warm water that sat on my bedside table. I noticed my pills there and concluded Robert had surmised my weakness had originated from a chronic condition that I'd suffered in Boston. I hadn't required these pills for months but had followed doctor's orders and carried them with me in case of a relapse. Never since arriving in Aspen Glen had I felt so completely drained as I did now.

Perhaps it was time to go home to the ranch, but how could I leave Robert alone? It was unthinkable. I'd simply have to be more careful. I popped a pill in my mouth and downed it with water. That should still the queasiness and give me a fresh start. Slowly I stood to my feet, but when the room started to sway, dropped back to a seated position. Strange that I felt grateful for the familiar signs of my previous condition and when my body ached all over I felt elated. These were not the same symptoms caused by the illness that the others suffered in the hospital, and I knew with a bit of rest I'd be fit as a fiddle.

"Thank you for standing guard. I believe I will be fine. I am going to lie down, and if you'd be so good as to check in with me again later, I'd appreciate it. I don't want to worry the doctor. He has so many others to attend to."

"I'll check every hour, Ma'am, till yer feeling yerself again." At that she closed the door and I watched as she slipped past the small window and out of sight.

I lay on my back and stared at the ceiling and asked the Lord for strength to do the job he sent me here to do. In the middle of the plea I drifted off.

It was late afternoon when I felt a presence in my room. I startled and out of habit, jumped to my feet. Robert stood staring at me wide eyed, and just in time he was there to once again catch me from toppling over. I relaxed into his embrace, and gazed into his eyes. He resembled a frightened deer. I summoned a brave smile to reassure him. I felt his strong arms tighten around me and for a moment I imagined he planned on kissing me. His lips quivered inches away, and then he backed off. I sighed, and rested my head against his shoulder. I caught a glimpse of a figure fleeing as it escaped the view of the small window. The intruder never appeared at the door before or after, so I chalked it off as a peeping Tom or Tammy, or most likely the young girl returning to check on me. There were lots of folks curious about the doctor and his so-called nurse. I focused again on Robert, and although I could feel his breath on my face, he felt detached. I'd have to make a better effort to solve the mystery of the good doctor. I attempted to once again affirm my composure. I failed, and the world went dark.

I spent two restless days in bed, hovering between sleep and wakefulness. The next time I fully awoke, my son, Patrick, relaxed on a nearby chair. Even in his sleeping position, I saw the concern written into the lines of his face. Coming to live at the ranch with him in the spring had saved my life, physically and emotionally, and I'd sworn to take care of myself so as to enjoy a long extended time with my son and his new wife. And soon Ruth Ellen's baby would be joining the family.

It was stupid of me to wear myself down to this point of exhaustion. I should have known better than to risk my health for such an extended period of time among the sick here in Stanton. But the need was so great. Even as this revelation attempted to balance the scales of guilt, I felt it creep in like a snake in the grass, condemning me of considering myself before others.

"Hello, PJ." I tried to sound more jovial than I felt.

He leapt to his feet and rushed over.

"Ma! You had me scared half to death." His face darkened as if he remembered that death was all around us. "I'm sorry. You've been through so much. I should have come earlier."

"As I recall, you did drop in once and I swished you away like a nuisance fly. I am sorry for not listening to your warnings."

"You assured me you'd be alright. Doc was supposed to watch out for you. I knew you wouldn't." His voice accused and I came to Robert's defense.

"PJ, you mustn't blame the doctor. He has had his hands full. It's a wonder that he hasn't collapsed from fatigue."

"While you were sleeping, there was a bit of breakthrough, Ma. Seems a rancher hereabouts sold some spoiled meat to a bunch of outlying farms. He suspected it might be tainted but hoped for the best. His family was starving and, of course, he didn't consider that a medical outbreak would result from his actions. He returned home Monday with his pockets full of money and a dead family to share it with. Seems his wife was too guilty to come and get help at the hospital, knowing they may be the cause of it all. He is repentant, but his neighbors are not taking his negligence well, and forgiveness is not on the horizon any time soon. Circuit judge is being brought in to hand out his sentence. Might be the only thing that's holding the grieving community from stringing him up."

A voice sounded from the doorway. It was Mr. Wright from the main house. Apparently, the fear that I'd pass the contagion along to his family had been resolved and he was comfortable standing in my proximity.

"Not any more," he said.

"What do you mean?" Patrick asked.

"Seems a bunch of men, got liquored and riled up, broke in to the holding cell, knocked the Deputy out cold and grabbed the prisoner. Took him to the hanging tree and served up their own kind of justice. Vengeance for their dead."

"What will happen when the judge arrives?" I asked.

"Deputy lost one of his own to the sickness, so he won't be pressin' charges with the mob for his bump on the head. The judge, well, he'll probably just pass on by and forget he was ever asked to sentence the guilty man. And the ones doing the grieving are mostly satisfied with the verdict."

"His entire family wiped out because of one bad decision."

"His wife and young'uns be better off dead than tryin' to live under the cursed man's shadow. No good man hereabouts woulda' taken his woman to live under his roof. The funeral's today. Most likely just the grave digger will be there."

"What of Reverend Tully? Surely he'll say some words before they bury them under?" I asked.

"Preacher be sprawled out on the floor at the hospital. Probably ate his fare share of the bad meat visitin' with parishioners. Nice of folks to feed him but his gut is objectin'. We be praying powerful hard fer him. He's the last of the Tulley's in Montana, far as I know."

The man was a bit too colorful in his description for my liking. "PJ, I need to go and see him."

"I did about an hour ago, Ma. The gravedigger and Tom was carrying him out on a stretcher."

"Oh, how dreadful," I groaned.

"But I hear the numbers are lessening now that they know the source. The doctor appears to have a better handle on the epidemic."

"That is great news." My joy was flawed by the news of the Reverend. He'd married Agnes and Stanley and blessed Patrick and Ruth Ellen after they recited their vows. We had good memories of the man, called home too early in his ministry to my way of thinking.

"No need for you to go back to that place, Ma. You are finished," Patrick said firmly as his eyes told me in no uncertain terms that he meant business. "I'll be taking you home with me, so don't even try to persuade me otherwise."

"I won't. I promise. I want to be around to see my grandchild born into this world."

"Yeah, and speaking of babies, Francine brought back a mid-wife from Boston – in fact, the very one that birthed Gerald. Can you believe that man is part of our family?"

"I can, and was thrilled to receive your wire telling me of the mystery of his heritage solved. I can't wait to see Francine. She must be over-the-top happy. And thank you for not waiting until your return to tell me. I'd have hated being the only one left in the dark about Ruth Ellen's new brother."

"Anyway, this mid-wife – Stacy's her name – has dabbled with other sicknesses over the years. She's helping the Doc right now and who knows if the hard-working man may inherit a real nurse in the deal." Patrick's face beamed. I'm sure it brought him a measure of peace to know two people in Aspen Glen who could deliver babies safely, just in case complications arose with Ruth Ellen.

"Doc could sure use a nurse," said the man at the door. "The man ain't gettin' any younger."

"Mr. Wright, you've hurt my feelings. Doctor Palatsie considered me a fine nurse and says he couldn't have made an impact here without my help." I pouted for effect and the man turned red.

He stammered with his response. "Never meant to imply ya didn't do a great job here, Ma'am."

"True enough! The more stories I hear about you, the more proud I am to call you Mother," Patrick said.

I laughed at their sudden awkwardness. "I'm teasing, boys. Nursing is not my calling. The midwife is welcome to take over my duties."

When Stacy Trop showed up a few minutes later to check on my recovery, a sudden uneasiness enveloped me. She was like a breath of fresh air as she spouted her contagious jovialness. High cheekbones shone rosy red and her full lips never turned downward once. She was definitely what this community needed to heal, but instead of that making me feel grateful, I felt selfishly jealous. No matter how I tried to shake my apprehension in this woman's appearance on the scene, the agitation continued. This was not like me – or so I thought.

Strange how ugliness within can hide its face and choose a time to appear when one is most vulnerable. I would not allow myself the excuse that my recent health issue presented. Stacy probably would have come to Stanton eventually. How could a real nurse not respond to such poverty of health? It was a calling and I thanked God for the position she would fill in the growing territory.

But, jealousy was wrong! Another scenario entered my wavering thoughts. Did I resent that she'd taken my place of service in the doctor's life? He'd have no further need to call on my assistance in the future. But no, that was not it! This had been the one and only time he'd asked me to accompany him. When the underlying truth hit me, I blushed. I was jealous that Robert's attention would now be divided. Competition! How can that be when I didn't even realize there was anything but friendship between us? He'd never once asked to court me, but that was no surprise given the inability for his tongue to conquer his fear of confrontation with a woman. How did I feel about the man? I'd never seriously entertained any thought beyond companionship.

I pulled back the sheet and swung my legs to the floor. I'd at least stand and face the woman head on. "Thank you, Stacy. I hear you and the doctor are busy with the last of the patients in the hospital."

"No newcomers all day. We are rejoicin' in that fact, to be sure," she said. "And now with ya up on your feet, the doctor'll stop worryin' and we can start workin' on findin' some smiles in this dreary place."

"Yes! I'm so glad you picked up on that. I think one of the hardest things to bear was to look on all the depressed faces that came through the hospital doors."

"Some folks are still not out of the woods, but there is hope in the air and each patient that walks out the door on their own two feet is a victory worth celebratin'." Stacy beamed, and I surrendered to her bubbling enthusiasm.

"Then I shall leave you and Doctor Palatsie to finish up here. I am overdue to go home." The thought of leaving here excited me more than I cared to admit. I turned to Patrick. "Has Agnes seen the construction site she called home before she left?"

"She has and she loves it."

"And Francine is home? I was so sorry to miss her and Daniel's wedding in Boston, and then the welcome home reception. But news filters to us over here, slow but sure. The grapevine, although not always completely accurate, is an unfailing source of information the world over."

I looked toward the door just as Mr. Wright man turned to leave.

"Please thank your dear wife for providing all those delicious meals – and miraculously none of the tainted meat," I said.

Patrick shouted "Amen to that!"

"Raise my own cow fer meat. Don't buy none from that scallywag," Mr. Wright said.

"Good news there. PJ, do you think we can send some meat over to help fill the smoke house again? We can guarantee it is prime beef, Mr. Wright, so you need not worry about it being tainted. The doctor and I have, no doubt, helped to deplete your food supply, and winter is close at hand."

Before the proud man could object, Patrick held up his hands. "No use refusing, neighbor. When Ma gets an idea you may as well just run with it. One of my men will deliver a prime Angus cow within a couple days fer you to use as you see fit."

"It's settled then. Now, let's go to the hospital, PJ, and say goodbye to Robert. I need to pick up the last of my things. I'm ready for the trip home."

"Are you sure, Ma? You just got out of bed," Patrick asked.

"All the more reason to leave now. No chance of me tiring out after all the sleep I've had." I chuckled as I swept past his objections and headed to what I referred to as my dressing room when it was actually a crate, chair, hooks on the wall and the revealing cracked mirror.

"My wife will pack you a light lunch to take," Mr. Wright said. He tipped his hat then hastened toward the main house.

I quickly threw the personal items that had made it to the shed into my bag and fastened the clasp shut. We walked slowly to the building we loosely called hospital. Today, the tired building somehow appeared brighter standing against the backdrop of a magnificent mountain and drenched in the rays of a noonday sun.

Perhaps new hope did have the power to change one's perception of everyday sights. That was a thought worth pondering. For there was hope in the air, and I could feel it penetrate my lungs and rejuvenate me.

Stacy had dashed on ahead and by the time Patrick and I entered the room that I'd learned to abhor over these past weeks, she and Robert were laughing over something on the workbench. His was a belly laugh, and in all the time I'd known him, I'd never heard him express joy quite this loudly. His one hand brushed her arm with an intimate gesture that I was not expecting so soon in their acquaintance.

Jealousy sprang to life and I felt like the intruder. I could not wait to flee the place.

Chapter 3

"What was that about?" Patrick asked after we'd started toward Aspen Glen.

"What?" I asked, pulling myself free from my torturous musing.

"You and Doctor Palatsie. You were downright cool toward him. I'd have thought after all that you two went through in Stanton we'd be hearing wedding bells in the near future."

"Don't be silly. You and Ruth Ellen would be lost without my interference in your life." I laughed clumsily and then sobered. "PJ, do you want me married and out of the homestead? I can find a place of my own if you two want the house for your own wee family. I'd completely understand, I could…"

"Ma, stop rambling! You know you will always be welcome in our home, whether there's just me and Ruthie or a whole parcel of young'uns to chase after."

"And cook for. You do know that your wife prefers to run wild with you on the ranch and leave kitchen detail to me."

"Unfortunately, I do. And I will need you to force her to stay home, at least until after the birthing. Rambunctious ranch duty might be too much right now. She doesn't move so fast anymore and could get injured easily. With that belly growing like it is, she'll soon be tripping over her own feet," Patrick said.

I laughed at his exaggeration. Ruth Ellen was carrying her child inside a tiny ball-shaped-belly that one would hardly notice from any other angle but the front.

"I will be glad to saddle her with some of the preserving. I high-jacked your cook while you were visiting in Boston and together we put down a lot of food for the winter months – to feed both the Jones' household and the hired men. But the bounty is plentiful and produce keeps piling up." My hand flew to cover my face. "Oh dear, I did leave Drake with a terrible mess of work to do alone." I opted not to tell Patrick of the flour-play disaster that I'd left him to clean alone.

"He had no need for help in the past. The man is competent. Came to the house the day after all the relatives arrived home and told us you weren't feeling well and that I should go and see for myself if I didn't believe him. Said his piece, then up and left without another word. Found it rather odd. Did he visit you in Stanton lately?"

"No, not that I recall. Perhaps it was when I was sleeping and someone else informed him that I was laid up."

"I was preparing to leave and head to Stanton anyway. Figured you'd done your time here and needed to come home. Sure enough, my fears that you'd overdo were founded, and I sat an entire day waiting for you to wake up."

"I apologized to everyone for pushing myself too hard. What more can I give, blood?"

"No, you best keep your own blood pumping inside," said Patrick. After a moment he spoke again. "So what all did you and Cook put up for winter?"

"Why do you call him Cook? He has a name, you know," I said.

"Suppose he does. Guess me and the boys just got used to calling him Cook."

"Well, it so happens that Drake and I made jams and jellies from every berry that came ripe for picking. Made relishes, sweet pickles and ones with garlic, and canned all kinds of fruit and vegetables from the gardens. My, but your men do plant a magnificent garden. And the fruit trees! A bit sparse, but Drake says we need to wait longer for a touch of frost for good sweet apples. I have great recipes that Drake is dying to squeeze out of me. A rather competitive sort, isn't he?"

"I wouldn't know." Patrick raised his eyebrows and couldn't hide the smirk from cracking out the corner of his lips. "Seems you know more about the man than I do."

"Nonsense. Simply answering your question," I said. "We'd just started on the corn when Robert came and whisked me away. There's still a lot of room in the root cellar for storing apples, potatoes and who knows what else I've missed. Of course, I made Drake put the onions in the dirt on the other side of the cellar. Can't imagine biting into an apple that's sat next to an onion for very long." I took a deep breath and rattled on. "This is my first year with such a great harvest to preserve. One thing I'm sure of is that we will not go hungry this winter. God has blessed this family and ranch."

Patrick agreed. "Yes, Ma'am! And I will thank him at every table gathering for bringing you home to Montana to live with us. I love you, Ma."

"You're getting awful mushy," I teased. "The young boy I remember steered clear of all forms of endearment whenever possible. But, I do hear that *mush* is a disease new fathers develop, especially when it's a baby girl."

"Don't let Ruth Ellen hear you say that. She's sticking to the boy theory and will hear nothing of ribbons and pigtails."

"In the end none of us have a choice. The Good Lord will

send whomever he sees fit and we'll be ecstatic either way." My voice trailed off. "A grandmother – I wonder if I'll be a good one."

"Perfect, no doubt." Patrick laid his hand on mine. "You still feeling all right, Ma?"

"Better than all right, Son. I'm suddenly quite eager to get back into my kitchen, preparing meals to keep our little mother healthy and happy."

Ruth Ellen flew out the door as soon as the buggy pulled in front of the homestead. She lifted her hand to help me down and when I cleared the carriage, Patrick clicked the horses into motion and headed toward the family barn.

Ruth Ellen clung to me. "Ma, we were so worried when we heard the news of your illness. Then you and PJ didn't come back for the longest time, and I felt sure I'd go stir-crazy waiting for word."

I patted her arm. "Don't you worry about me, daughter." I'd always wanted a second child and had hoped for a girl but Albert would have none of it. Said one brat to feed was enough. From the moment I'd met Patrick's wife in Boston I'd considered her as my own flesh and blood. Anyone with half an eye could see the young couple were meant for one another. And the way she looked at my boy... well, I just knew she'd make him the happiest man in all of Montana for the rest of his life. And sure enough, she was off to a roaring start by carrying his first baby – their first baby, and my first grandbaby. Life was good.

My knees buckled slightly, cramping after such a long sit, but I corrected my posture before Ruth Ellen noticed the weakness.

"If you don't mind, I could use a rest. Then I'll get up and help you with the dinner preparations."

"No need to help. I've got it all ready cooking in the oven. PJ's favorite – roasted beef from the Jone's stock, baby-sized potatoes and carrots from the cellar, and home made bread to sop up the gravy."

I laughed. "PJ has many favorite dishes and that is certainly one. I'll be down in a bit. Why don't you run to the barn and talk to the animals with your husband."

"Oh, Ma, you know me too well. I love this ranch and the life your son has given me."

"Well, run along then. I can still mount the steps by myself."

Despite my claim to healing fame, Ruth Ellen waited until I topped the landing before she ran out the door. I walked to my room and lay full out on the bed. It was so comfortable. Although the cot in Stanton was much preferred over a space on the hospital floor, it had been lumpy, managing to meet the needs of an exhausted worker, but far from the luxurious mattress in my own room at the Jones Star ranch. I sighed and closed my eyes.

A vision of Robert's laughing face staring into Stacy's well-rested and jubilant features taunted me, and just before I lost consciousness, my mind switched and conjured up a picture of Drake – the cook. He was indeed so much more than that, and I sincerely hoped that PJ realized this man's worth. Faithful employees were hard to find. Then darkness blocked out both men and I fell into a deep sleep.

Ruth Ellen brought a plate of food to me hours later. I heard her gentle knock and watched her put the tray on the table. She poured my tea and stepped back to see if I was awake. "We didn't want you to sleep all night with nothing in your tummy but a light lunch on the run. Feel free to indulge tonight and rest in your rooms. We will catch up on all the news in the morning."

She planted a quick kiss on my cheek and left the room.

I appreciated her thoughtfulness, for not only was my body weary, but my mind and emotions had been taxed to the limit. To look death in the face, hear stories of families left with no father, and still others relieved to dig theirs six feet under, had left me speechless many times over. I'd seen little of that first woman, Bessie, who'd shared the step with me after her husband's name had marked death number one on our list of fatalities. She'd listened patiently to my condolences and the message of healing while donning a weird sense of duty and ritual. The next time I'd caught a glimpse of her was when her supposed *man-in-waiting* was brought in with the same sickness, and despite her avid attentiveness to his demands he treated her with scorn. His foul mouth had reminded me of my bout with verbal abuse from Patrick's father. I'd broken free of dependence on men after his death, and had determined not to make the same mistake twice. It had pained me to watch Bessie, as a widow of one day, willing to throw her lot in with an equally abusive man and live the same hell over and over again. Perhaps I should have talked more with her when she walked a second time behind a closed casket. They'd passed by the hospital on way to the cemetery and my heart ached for her loss. Not for the men in her life, but for life itself.

  I nibbled at the tasty meal and finally pushed the last quarter of it away. I couldn't eat another bite if I planned on sleeping through the night. Patrick was standing in the hallway ready to knock when I opened the bedroom door to place the tray on the floor outside. He swung the bath pan to-and-fro with a grin plastered on his face.

  "Any takers? Thought you might appreciate a bath before you retire. I'll bring the water up if you're game."

  "I would love to sink into a tub of soapy warm water but I can come to the bathing room downstairs. It's a lot of trips up here with pails of water."

  He laughed. "It would be my privilege to spoil the lady who has given so much of herself to help the sick."

  "Next you're going to tell me that you need the exercise," I said. "I will come downstairs shortly and enjoy your treat in the lovely room you built for such a purpose."

He tipped his head in my direction. "As you wish. The pouring will commence abruptly, so make yourself ready."

Inside my room I rummaged through the dresser drawer and pulled out a soft cotton gown. At the dressing table I stopped to turn up the wick in the lantern. I stared in the mirror at the ghost of a woman's image. My deep brown eyes had lost their touch with the stars and appeared dreary and sad. My lips were chapped and swollen from lack of moisture in the sickroom environment. I removed the pins from my hair and brushed the lengths until all the tats were gone. With a final grunt of disapproval, I opened another drawer and removed a scrub cloth, a bar of fragrant soap and a huge towel. Last thing in my hand was the lantern as I turned and left my bedroom.

Downstairs, I found the tub filled with water, warm to the touch and inviting with bubbles and a sweet aroma of roses. I removed the dress I'd been wearing for two days and threw it in the corner before stepping into the water. I sunk as low as I could, hugged my legs and rested my head on my knees. I sat still for a long while and savored the pleasure. Eventually I gripped the bar of soap and scrubbed my body with the washcloth, wishing that somehow the scars left on my heart could be wiped clean as easily. I sank lower and my head went under. When it emerged, I lathered my hair, digging my fingers into the itchy scalp, and then plunging beneath the surface again. I rolled my head and ran fingers through to remove as much soap as possible. I reached for the last clean pitcher of water, stood to my feet and let it flow over my head and cascade down my re-energized body.

Stepping from the tub, I dried and then guided the nightgown over my head and shoulders and felt it fall gently to the floor to cover my ankles. I wrapped my hair in the towel and picked up the lantern. The rest could wait for morning. Bed was calling my name and I was ready.

The next day I was awake before the rooster crowed. I flew from the bed, picked one of my nicer work dresses from the wardrobe and hurried into it. At the dressing table I worked the mangle of curls into submission and wound them into a knot at the back of my head. At the front I plucked a few strands from captivity and after twirling it between my fingers allowed it to tumble in reckless abandonment close to my face. A gentler touch helped to soften the fine lines of aging that seemed to deepen and spread anew every day. Preparing to face the day was time consuming, when all I wanted was to throw my face into the morning sun and shout *amen* to the world. *So be it* was today's resolution and it felt good to place the ills of the world in the Lord's hands and leave them there.

In the kitchen all was quiet but for the sound of a gentle perk from the coffee simmering on the stove. That would be Patrick's morning contribution, letting his ladies sleep in while he stole off to work. I poured a cup and made my way to the front porch. The rocking chair welcomed me with open arms and I sank into the relic, a gift from a distant Jones grandfather. The chair and the chest had been Patrick's only request when he headed West many years ago. It seemed like another lifetime, but in truth, only seven years, or maybe eight. I smiled – losing track of time was definitely a sign of growing older.

With my head lowered while sipping the hot brew, I missed hearing the footsteps on the porch beside me until he stood there. I jumped and spilled some of the liquid on my clean dress.

"Sorry, didn't mean to startle ya none," Drake said.

His hands reached forward, as if to help me wipe the stain away, then quickly reversed. He pushed them into his pockets and his stiffened arms held them there.

"Drake, " I said. "How nice of you to drop by."

"The boys are done breakfast, and all's left to do is wash up and get started on lunch. Thought I'd slip away and see how ya was doin' now that yer home again."

"I am doing fine, Drake. Extremely happy to wake up at the ranch this morning and thrilled that the epidemic in Stanton is winding down. The doctor should soon be back in his office."

"Hear he got his wish fer a nurse," he said while shuffling his feet and not making eye contact.

"Stacy will indeed be a great asset to him. His patient load has grown far too large for one man to do alone. Her coming to Aspen Glen is timely," I said, knowing that speaking the truth would help to send any remaining jealousy into the mountains to hide.

Drake grunted and changed the subject. "Got time for some cannin' this afternoon? The corn is piling up, and I got the boys to husk some for me last night."

"Of course," I said, casting a teasing glance his way. "Pick up where we left off, right?" He grunted again and avoided my scrutiny, although I thought I caught a glimpse of a smile that he chose to hold at bay. Perhaps he was remembering our flour-fight before I left for Stanton. And perhaps he was as embarrassed as me. "Are you okay, Drake?"

"Sure. Why shouldn't I be? I'll be going down to the mess hall now. See you there – around two?"

"I'll be there." I thought I'd eliminate the chance that the foolhardy episode stood between us. "Wearing a clean apron. No flour needed for corn, right?"

That set his biggest smile free and as he beamed, I remained confused. If not the escapade with the flour, then what was causing the underlying dissention between us?

"Cleaned up yer mess. Ya owe me big time, woman," he said. His entertaining chuckle sounded like music to my ears.

The Drake I had grown to appreciate reappeared and I relaxed. It appeared we were back on track.

"I'll see you sharp at two o'clock, sir, after I clean this stain on my dress that you caused." I stood and looked him square in the eyes. "Guess that makes the debt even."

I swished past him and went inside the house. When the door closed I smiled and all felt fine in my world. I chanced a peek out the side window and saw the man heading down the path toward his work place. He looked back, and then I saw the alteration – first in the drooped shoulders and then in the tired kick at the loose dirt. Turning toward the path, he trudged on, and again confusion settled in my heart. I'd been so pleased to call him my friend, but somehow I'd hurt him and he wasn't sharing. Try as I might I could not recall how or when such an incident had occurred. This afternoon I'd place a greater effort into bridging the gap that separated us.

Chapter 4

"Spit it out because I will not stand here another minute and listen to the words you are not saying!"

The corn slipped in my hand and the knife sliced my knuckle. A tear escaped, more from frustration than any pain the cut caused. Drake sped into motion. He threw me a clean cloth.

"Wrap it tight. I'll be right back."

By the time he returned with his medical box I was feeling light-headed. He guided me to the pump and braced me against the counter before he unwrapped my shoddy effort with the cloth.

"What part of tight didn't you understand?" He was scolding me but he smiled and spoke gently. "Take it easy, Clare. It's a long way from yer heart."

"Don't make fun of me. I feel foolish enough," I said.

"No need. Cut myself many a time preparin' food. It's the sign of a good cook."

"Don't flatter me either. I'm not in the mood."

"Tut, tut…" When he was satisfied the wound was clean, he wrapped one arm around my shoulder and ushered me into a nearby chair. He then knelt down in front of me. "You were sayin' somethin' about speakin' yer mind?"

"Not me! I have no trouble saying it like it is. But you – well, you are the most private and insufferable man I've ever encountered!"

"And ya don't know how to handle that. Good to hear. Cause we don't need two of us spoutin' off at the drop of a hat."

I clicked my tongue in annoyance. Standing my ground and demanding truth from Drake had backfired horribly. "Why won't you tell me what's bothering you, Drake. I thought we were friends."

"Friends?" He raised his eyebrows and buried his head in medicating the torn area and laying the flap of skin flat again. He took a new strip of cloth and began to wrap my hand. "Should be stitching it, but yer probably not up fer my sewing skills. Leave ya scarred fer life."

"If it needs stitches, do it and stop blathering about pretty hands."

He smiled. "No, I think you will get away with wrapping it tight." He emphasized this by pulling it extra tight.

"Thanks for the gentle touch, Dr. Drake."

"Yer welcome. Why don't you sit still and have a glass of lemonade."

"Why don't you join me and start talking? If I have to suffer the shame of making a fool of myself with a careless slice to the knuckle, surely I can have my way in the thing that caused it."

"Like a bad temper?"

"You are infuriating! All I want is a little honesty. I know you well enough to know you are hiding something from me. Spit it out now, or I shall go home and let you wallow in it forever."

He all but laughed at my stance. "I used that line with the schoolyard boys when I was a kid – give me my way or I'll take my marbles and go home."

My mood bubbled with fury, too close to boiling point. "Childish? You are implying that I'm behaving like a child." I stood to my feet more embarrassed than ever. "This has gone all wrong. I'm sorry Drake. I think I should go home."

He tipped my chin upward until our eyes locked and then gathered both of my hands in his. "What do you want to know, lovely lady? That I was annoyed when you abandoned everythin' we were doin' in the Jones kitchen and ran off with another man, or that when I heard of your illness in Stanton and rushed to see you, I found you in the doctor's arms." I gasped. "Which do you think hurt and confused me the most?"

I stammered. "I don't understand. Why should you care? We just cook together."

"That bullet numbers three. They just keep comin'." He allowed my hands to drop to my sides and walked to the counter. "Lesson learned. Not all words should pass the lips."

Now I had no words – none I felt safe uttering at this moment. Drake was jealous. He felt the same way I did when encountering Robert with Stacy. My thoughts raced. Where is that fine line between friendship and something deeper? And how do you recognize it in someone else or know when one's slipped across the set boundaries? I could not deny my feelings for Robert, however unclear they were, but this afternoon all I wanted was to restore the relationship with Drake, back to the same level that we'd shared before I left for Stanton.

"I don't know what to say, except I don't remember you being in Stanton and I don't recall..." Then it hit me. I had been in Robert's arms, once, in the shanty when I fell ill. He caught me when I felt faint, but I'd liked it, even thought he would kiss me. How could I deny that? Drake would see right through me.

"Ah, yer memory returns." He washed his hands under the pump and with his back to me, continued to speak. "Perhaps you should go see what PJ thinks of yer cut. He'd gladly cart ya to see the good doctor fer stitches."

"You know very well the doctor has not returned to Aspen Glen. You are just trying to get rid of me." Yelling helped to dissipate the floundering drama taking place on my insides.

Drake's tone remained steady and firm. "The time has come to say goodbye, Clare. It was fun while it lasted, but now the family is home and life goes on. Perhaps ya should go with the flow."

"Whose flow? I am not a puppet that you can manipulate. You are the most confusing, exasperating person." I inhaled deeply as I recalled this same conversation with Albert many years previous. The memory clinched it. "Drake – I don't even know your last name - but understand this, I refuse to walk that unstable road beyond friendship with another unpredictable man. Marriage number one was enough for me!"

He turned and faced me – the darkest eyes boring into my deepest hurts. "The last name is Whitfield, and I don't recollect invitin' ya to walk down the aisle with me."

My endurance boiled over, and I fled the room while a thousand ghosts chased me along the path toward home. Tears blinded me – tears I could neither control or identify the source. Inner confusion muddled into a central mass - Drake, Robert and Albert – all spinning webs of pain, hardship and love.

I stumbled into the house and headed for the stairs. In my room I paced the floor until the beat of my heart settled into an easy rhythm. I sat at my dressing table and looked into the large mirror that revealed all. My cheeks held a mix of a deep rosy shade blended into the suntan that had developed over the summer. Montana demanded more outside activities than Boston had, and even while cooped up in the Stanton hospital, I'd escaped the foul air as often as the patients had allowed. Now, in the confines of my room – free from the stress men inflicted –

the fine lines around my angry eyes smoothed and my face visibly relaxed. I needed to regroup and gain back control of my life. Trouble was I couldn't pinpoint a time when I'd lost it.

Life had been simpler when all this emotional baggage lay buried, with no desire of resurrection. It had been easy to live in isolation, coming out of my shell when I chose and climbing back in when the going got tough. That was the easy solution – leave it all buried. After all, I loved my life with Patrick and Ruth Ellen, had developed new friendships, and was busy with ranch and town events. That should be enough for any woman of my age. Why suffer this emotional turmoil speculating on a man – any man. My deceased husband, Albert, had filled my life with ups and downs, spiraling my emotions into whirlwinds of instability. Did I want that again?

Drake was a mystery. I saw it in his eyes – a past that hindered his present. Yet I felt confident he'd never considered his history as a hindrance that affected his future. On one hand he confessed he wants more, perhaps even with me, but then he shuts us down with that rude comeback about marriage. A defense mechanism? Perhaps he was no more capable of handling anything other than friendship than I was. I'd never considered us growing beyond companions with a common interest, and selfishly wanted that to remain intact. He'd sparked spontaneity into my life and I'd gobbled it up like a gourmet feast for my soul. But to consider a deeper commitment required burying the ghosts – on both sides.

Vulnerability was something I'd guarded against all my married life with Patrick's father, and today I'd encountered it again, head on with Drake. Nothing would ever be the same between us. I needed to face that and move on.

An image of Robert popped into my head. What of him? He would be easier to live with – should I decide in that direction. He was a kind, decent man who led a well-disciplined life. Every day upon awakening, he knew his mission, and he loved providing the community with his services as doctor. He was fulfilled and perhaps not even looking for a wife – although his attention toward me since my arrival in Aspen Glen suggested otherwise. The sight of his close proximity to Stacy in the hospital flashed through my mind but I dismissed her from the debate. Robert was not one to jump into the fire, and his new nurse burned hot like a blaze out of control. A life with Robert, would involve constant abandonment to serve his patients – that picture appeared a rather lonely existence. If I chose him, I would miss my family, watching them grow, and meeting their everyday needs. And feeling indispensible was important to me. *Here I go again.* The doctor had never even kissed me when given the opportunity.

What was this crazy debate about anyway? I sounded like I had a choice – as if either man had even suggested courting me. No one was beating down my doors looking for a wife. I ordered myself to back down and stop this useless musing. I'd make a stand, right now. No men in the foreseeable future. I'd stick to female friendships. Surely, that was less complicated. Yes, the baby was soon coming, and it would be a full time job being a grandmother and looking after my growing family. I stood to my feet. Settled! Staying healthy and content must become my main focus from here on in.

Downstairs I busied myself with preparations for dinner. I wanted it to be special. As if my new resolution dictated that I perfect my skills for this family that I'd chosen to serve the rest of my life. And, sure enough, today's rewards fed that commitment. Patrick could not stop licking his lips and raving about the meal, and Ruth Ellen's gratefulness at having the ranch kitchen performing at top notch, gave her the freedom she desired to work in the barns and ride the hills.

Then I recalled my son's request, that I encourage his wife

to stay inside and protected until the baby was born.

"Ruth Ellen, dear. Do you suppose you could remain at the homestead tomorrow to help me husk corn and can it? I went and cut myself today and it makes the job a bit awkward."

Patrick jumped to his feet. "I almost forgot the box sitting on the porch. Drake must have carried it up for you to put in our pantry."

Ruth Ellen squealed when she saw the jars of preserved corn. "Look, now you won't have to do it tomorrow, right?"

I looked at Patrick and raised my eyebrows. Too late he picked up on my plan to bushwhack his wife and keep her inside for the day.

"Now Ruthie, there's a good lot of corn done, but it's a long winter and wouldn't you like to have a buttery taste come next spring?"

Ruth Ellen exaggerated a pout. "I suppose. Do you think Chance will miss me?"

"How about you and I go for a short ride tomorrow evening after I finish chores? That is, if you're not too tired after preserving all day," he said.

"Oh, I wont be, PJ. I promise," Ruth Ellen said with enthusiasm. Sometimes I wondered if she were the child. Regardless, motherhood would mature her soon enough.

"Good then – tomorrow is settled," I said.

"Ma, don't you tire of having every day settled for you? I prefer to live in the spur-of-the-moment and squeeze life in around the work."

I laughed. "Or in your case, the work around life."

"Never truer spoken words," Patrick said as he stood and planted a kiss on his wife's cheek.

"I'm off to do chores. Why don't you rest up Ruthie, and we'll all play a game when I come in."

"A game! What game?" She began to ramble on about the

many choices stored in the cupboard when her husband interrupted.

"Slow down, woman. You choose. Surprise us, okay?"

She jumped to her feet. "Be right back, Ma, to help with the dishes. I'll set up the parlor table. I know exactly the one we will play."

A week later, on a similar evening when the three of us had just settled in the parlor with our hot tea and evening treat, a knock sounded at the door. I jumped to my feet.

"You two relax. I'll see who it is."

I hurried to the door and opened it to find Robert standing there with a bouquet of fresh cut flowers. He passed them to me and smiled.

"Back from Stanton and couldn't think of anyone I wanted to see more than you. Picked these from my garden in town. It needs some loving attention, mind ya, but these here blossoms were right pleased to be picked out from the mess of weeds strangling them from all sides."

"Thank you, Robert. This was very thoughtful of you."

"Not nearly enough of a thank you for all the help you gave me at the hospital. I'm beholden to you."

So that was it. It was payback for my contribution to his medical emergency. Oh, well, they were still beautiful. "You do not need to feel obligated to me in any way. I enjoyed helping you."

"Enjoyed being a rather stretch of the imagination, I dare say," he said.

I laughed. "Yes, agreed. An enormous stretch. Please come in and have tea with us. We just retired to the parlor."

He removed his hat. "Thank you. A cup of tea would hit the spot about now. There's finally a cool breeze in the evening air. Maybe the heat of summer is bidding us goodbye at long last."

"I hope it holds up for the church picnic on Sunday."

"Suppose that marks the end of the holiday season. Kids will be back to school as soon as all the harvest is in," Robert said as he hung his sweater and hat on the hook by the door.

"Thank you for reminding me. I need to plan some games for the children at the picnic. Got busy with the food preparation for the family and forgot I volunteered to keep the youngsters busy for an hour. How on earth can I occupy them for an entire hour? Perhaps I bit off more than I can chew. But all the other women on the committee are so busy in their homes."

"I'd be glad to help if you like. I've been present for a number of church picnics and stitched many ambitious young lads after tumbling from the limb of a tree."

Oh," I groaned. "Then we definitely will not include any tree games. I do not want to put the doctor to work on his day off."

"Hopefully, my day off. My schedule can change in a heartbeat," he said. I noticed his gaze penetrate me and saw questions hovering behind his eyes.

"Yes, I suppose so. But life shouldn't be lived in a box, right?" Where did that come from? Not from my resolution to live the routine existence I'd settled into.

"Clare, I..."

Patrick entered the hallway. "Doctor, what a pleasant surprise. Those flowers meant to butter Ma up," he said as he slapped the man on the back.

"A thank you for all her hard work, and because she deserves a bouquet, don't you think?" Robert said as he winked at me.

The man was brave when others were looking on. "Excuse me. I'll put these in water and bring an extra cup into the parlor. Patrick, please take our guest into the other room."

I walked into the kitchen just as a blushing smile reached

my lips. Flowers – when was the last time a man had brought me flowers. Never, I decided with a touch of sadness. And never simply because he thought I deserved it and appreciated me. That made the gift all that more significant. Robert appeared to have lost a thousand pounds of worry off his shoulders since the last time I saw him and the shaven whiskers gave him a younger appearance. Fanning and criss-crossing the stems in the bottom of the vase created a beautiful display. I filled the glass container with water and decided to bring it in the parlor so we could all enjoy them. I grabbed an extra cup, removed my apron and straightened my wrinkled dress. As I passed by the hallway mirror, I pinched color in my cheeks and smiled. A man caller, unplanned and unwanted, but it fed my vanity nonetheless.

I entered the room as the occupants burst into laughter. It appeared to be a private joke for no one chose to let me in on the conversation leading up to the jovial outburst. I poured tea into the cup and passed it to Robert who had settled on the settee. Patrick and Ruth Ellen snuggled in the one opposite him and I looked for an alternate place to sit.

Robert tapped the seat beside him. "Don't be shy, Clare. After all, we did share the same bed for a few weeks."

I glanced at Patrick in horror. "Not at the same time! Really Robert, you need to curb your tongue."

They all laughed again. I perched on the edge of the seat and slid backward until my spine touched the flowery cushions of the sofa behind me. If I moved my arm at liberty it would rub against Robert's, so I held the one on his side tight against my ribs. He was not so cautious in his movements. More than once I felt the brush of his jacket against my shirtsleeve.

When the teapot was empty and the goodies all nibbled away, Patrick spoke. "Well, old man, get to it before we all grow too old to hear the words."

Robert cleared his voice and inched forward in his seat.

He turned his full attention toward me, and I held my breath as I felt the air in the room being sucked clear out the open window. I glanced at Patrick and Ruth Ellen whose faces beamed from ear to ear. Robert's expression held fear and his voice trembled when he spoke.

"Clare, this announcement is long overdue but I have spoken with your son and he has given permission for me to ask you." He stopped and seemed unable to continue.

I decided to help the poor man. "Ask me what, Robert?"

He took my hand and I felt the cold sweat from his fingers slide with mine. He appeared to only then notice the small bandage I still wore from my episode with the knife at the mess hall.

"Your hand? What did you do to your hand?" Robert asked.

I let out the breath I'd been holding, while Patrick and Ruth Ellen's faces, turning a light shade of blue from their pent-up anticipation of the question, nearly exploded.

"My hand? Just a battle with a knife. It's healing fine," I said.

Patrick interrupted. "Get it over with, man, before we all die of suspense."

Robert blurted it out before he lost nerve. "I'd like to call on you. Maybe court you for a spell until the notion of speaking our vows settles in deeper-like."

Was that a marriage proposal?

My first husband, Albert, had wined and dined me until I was so dizzy I'd said yes.

I did not have that excuse today – my head was indeed clear of any emotional manipulation in this moment. The faces of the three eager participants in the room glistened with joy and that is what tipped the scales for me. What else could I say but yes when my family appeared so eager for me to be happy? And to them *happy* meant married. And Robert, the only man left standing, had finally rallied a brave start at romance.

Time stood still and my voice blurted out the answer. "Why Robert, everyone has expected you to call on me for ages. What took you so long?" Answer a question with a question – was that a real commitment? I did not have any time to ponder it.

Robert pulled me to my feet and planted a warm kiss on my cheek. "It's official then. That's a load off my chest."

Patrick and Ruth Ellen shoved in to congratulate us. Somewhere along the way I got caught up in the excitement, and my resolution to remain single to my dying day flew out the window with my last breath of fresh air.

Chapter 5

We went on our first buggy ride later that evening. Robert updated me on all the news of the final week at the hospital. The ladies from the community volunteered to come in afterwards and do the big clean. I was grateful not to be there for that event. Even though we kept the floors as clean as possible, a residue remained that I felt sure would never go away.

"The Wright's received PJ's gift just before we left. They were quite teary eyed and said to tell y'all how grateful they were. Good folks they turned out to be."

I smiled. "Not like others that we crossed paths with in Stanton. I met my share of women with very different ideas on how to live life and raise their children. Very backward compared to the people I've met here in Aspen Glen."

"You are attempting to be kind. Some were downright peculiar and unhealthy if you want my opinion."

"Thank you. It helps to know that I was not judging solely from my worldview. I would hate for someone to consider me snobbish," I said.

"You, my dear, could never be considered snobbish." He

placed a tender hand on my knee but quickly looked to see if that met with my approval.

"Pray tell, Robert. How do mature people behave during this courting session? I am ignorant in the ways of the West and feel nervous venturing outside my comfort zone."

"It did seem easier when we could just be ourselves and not worry about the right and wrong of it all," he said.

"Then let's just make it so. We already have a good foundation of friendship and understanding of what makes us tick – don't we?" I asked.

"I'm pretty easy to please. Lead a simple life," Robert said.

"A very busy life."

"Will that be a problem?" he asked.

"To be honest, I'm not sure. Whatever will I find to do in that tiny space you call home while you're working? I was looking forward to spoiling my new grandchild."

"Regret saying yes already?"

"You are a good man, Robert. Let's not talk this to death," I said growing uneasy in the direction the conversation was headed.

I desired honesty, but at the same time feared it. Besides, everyone would be so disappointed. The doctor and I had been coupled off from day one. And with my mind in the constant upheaval it was these days, probably I should depend on others who saw a clearer picture of what was best for me.

Robert walked me to the door and tipped his hat. "You've made me very happy tonight, Clare. I'm scheduled to go backcountry, but I'm free day after tomorrow. Can you meet me at the Diner for lunch?"

"I'm sure PJ will let me use the buggy. Yes, I'll be there at noon." Inside I felt ecstatic for the opportunity to drop in on Agnes, see how the newlyweds were getting on and get another peek at her new place.

"Perfect. Until then," he raised my hand to his lips and ended up kissing the bandage. He smiled and blushed. "Goodnight, Clare."

He mounted his buggy and drove off. Our courtship had not even received the seal of a decent kiss. Even a tiny peck on the lips would have sufficed. Maybe I was placing too much value on a kiss. I'm sure he'd get around to it. I'd hoped that it might help cement the decision in my heart that I'd declared with my mouth – to be the doctor's wife. *Mrs. Clare Palatsie* I tested the sound of the name. Perhaps it had a unique ring. Jones was so... plain.

It wasn't until I stepped inside the house that I realized Stacy Trop's name had never once been mentioned, even while he recited all the happenings in Stanton after my departure. Surely a trained nurse would have been a better lifetime choice for a partner than I could ever hope to be. Yet, I received the flowers and the proposal. How odd. I wondered if she'd agreed to help him with his practice. For his sake, I hoped yes. For my sake, I wasn't sure I'd want to hear all the colorful stories of Stacy and the doctor every night at supper. Envious again? In light of my new status in Robert's life, jealousy was an unnecessary burden to carry. He'd chosen me and that was that.

"Well, how was the first evening of being betrothed to the good doctor?"

"PJ, you didn't have to wait up for me? Save your late-night concerns for the daughter you are so certain Ruth Ellen is carrying. She will cause you many sleepless nights in the future."

"Mm... I was expecting to see a glow on your face when you walked in, but nothing. Are you happy, Ma? I know we've teased and thrown you two together since the first dance here at the homestead. Doesn't mean you have to marry the man."

"I thought you were thrilled tonight when he asked to court me?"

"I'm only thrilled if you are."

"It was a surprise, to be sure. Not at all what I expected."

"What did you expect?"

"The flowers were a nice touch. Not used to such an intimate gift from a man, but he caught me off guard with the other. We are terrific friends and I cherish that. Many have wed with less than that for a start."

"I don't particularly care about *the many* out there. I care about you and your happiness."

"I'm easy to please." As soon as I said it I recalled Robert saying the exact same words.

"Mm… Another solid base for a successful union." He stood to his feet. "Keep searching your heart, Ma. You'll come up with the right reason before you walk down the aisle."

"You're right, of course. This courtship could go on till spring at least. Yes, that would be perfect. I'll have months to watch the baby grow. And I'll be able to help Ruth Ellen get your wee family settled into a good routine before I leave."

"Stay as long as you want." He kissed me lightly on the cheek, lit an extra lantern for me and headed toward the stairway. "Time to join my wife upstairs. Sleep tight, Ma."

I watched after him until he became a fleeting shadow disappearing down the hall to his room. I filled the coffee pot and stood it ready for the first person awake in the morning to heat on the stove. At the window, my gaze lingered on the half-moon rising to take its rightful place in the sky. The urge to watch its progress consumed me as I picked up the lantern and stepped outside. I loved to watch the familiar night show in the sky. Usually before bed, the family prayed together to the Creator of the stars – but not tonight. I stood alone and wondered if it were a sign that I'd soon no longer be a part of the Jones family tradition. It saddened me and I petitioned God with a heart of confusion to guide my steps.

The night before my luncheon with Robert, I had a restless sleep, followed by a long morning alone in the kitchen. Ruth Ellen was dilly-dallying at the barn again. She knew I had plans to go to town and should be in the kitchen preparing lunch for her husband. I decided to drive the carriage around that way before heading to Aspen Glen. That girl needed to get her head on straight and be about her womanly duties. I found her accosting one of Patrick's men about not returning the feed bin to its proper corner. When he left I approached her.

"Do you really think it's your responsibility to call out your husband's employees?" I asked.

"He's said more than once that the ranch and everything in it belongs to both of us. He doesn't expect me to be a doormat, Ma."

"I understand that, but the men expect PJ to do the reprimanding. Perhaps telling him first would be a better way to handle misdemeanors."

She plunked on a stool and looked at me with big scared eyes. "Oh Ma, I'm such a grouch on the inside these days that it leaks out of my mouth like water pumped from the well. I'm terrified that I will hate being a mother. The ranch has such a strong pull for me and the baby will take much of my time."

"All of your time, my dear. Especially after I marry Robert."

I saw the tears gather in the corner of her eyes. "I'm a terrible person. Why does Patrick love me so much?"

"Who knows a man's heart? I just know he fought hard for you after the accident that stole your memory of him. Leads me to believe that he must have liked being married to you and did not want it to end. It's all a woman can ask for in this life – to be so unconditionally loved by a man."

"Like you and Doctor Palatsie. Ma, I am pleased you've found happiness in Aspen Glen," Ruth Ellen said.

"I found happiness a long time before Robert entered the picture – in you and PJ. The doctor is a bonus kind of love."

Even I wasn't sure what that statement meant. A man's love should not be a bonus. I'd always dreamed it would be everything – a reason to wake in the morning, go to bed at night and everything in-between. A woman took pride in her own home, a man to love and look after. Even living in a dutiful union with Albert, I'd taken pride in what belonged to us – my kitchen, our small family, and providing nourishment for them. All as it should be. I wondered if I'd simply transferred this duty to PJ's family. That would not be a healthy environment for any of us. Yes, I realized the need to be gone from Jones Star Ranch – to let the young ones make their own future.

Then my eyes caught a movement at the open doorway and Drake stood staring at me as if I had two heads.

"Drake," I called out. "How are you doing?"

"Fine."

Ruth Ellen cut in. "If you two will excuse me I'll be headed to the house. Time is marching on and that bread won't bake itself."

"That's the spirit," I said as she passed by. "See you later."

As soon as she was gone from sight Drake spoke again. "Noticed you get out of the buggy and thought I'd pop over and congratulate you."

"Congratulate me?" It took a moment and then it sunk in. "You've heard already?"

"The ranch grapevine is a wonderful thing. Not much happens at the big house that slips by us down here."

I stammered – not sure how I felt about Drake congratulating me on my betrothal to another man. Not after him baring his heart then ordering me from his presence all in the same quarrel.

Thank you." I glanced down and shuffled my feet. "It is

probably not appropriate to say, but I miss working in the kitchen with you. It's rather lonely at times."

"Won't be lonely fer long. When's the big day?" he asked.

"Oh, not for a long time," I spouted a little too eagerly. I bit my lip.

Did that sound like procrastination? Whatever would the man think of me?

I needn't have worried about that. For unlike Robert, Drake chose today to loosen his tongue, despite his resolve to refrain from heart-stomping honesty in my presence. I sensed a new ease spilling from him and cringed at the realization that I no longer threatened his heart. So, let the words rip – he'd have no reason for regret.

"Sounds like yer wantin' to wait till after the baby is born."

"Yes! That's it entirely. I am so looking forward to being a grandmother. Does that sound foolish to you?"

"Not at all. You'll make a fine one."

"Drake, I feel like we parted on bad terms and I..."

"No need to fret. I've learned to move on, as you apparently have."

I ignored his latter cut to the marrow and addressed the first. "You've been disappointed in love that many times," I smiled trying to bring the tease back into our conversation. That had been a comfortable fit, not this awkward standoff.

"Was married once," Drake said.

"Oh, I never knew. What happened to your wife?" I asked.

"Someone burnt the house with her in it when I was off hunting."

"Oh, Drake, that's terrible! Did you have children?"

"A boy. Suppose he was burnt too. Hard to tell. All the ashes looked the same." As he relayed the story his voice sounded detached and his expression unreadable.

My heart was in my throat and I couldn't utter a word. He brought the discussion to a close.

"Long time ago. I got over it and moved on," Drake said.

"Did you never find the person responsible for setting the fire?"

"I know who did the killing. No justice to be had there." He pushed away from the doorframe. "Now that ya know my sordid past ya can rest easy. Ya made the right decision goin' with the doctor. He's a sure package, tied in a nice bow waiting fer you to unwrap. Good day to ya, Clare."

Then he was gone and I couldn't move due to the emotional load he'd just dumped on me. I leaned against a nearby wall and let the silent tears trickle down my cheeks. Drake claimed to have put his family's death behind him, but it was obvious he had not healed from the ordeal. That saddened me, and still, the wall between us stood stronger than ever. Then he'd slammed the door by offering his best wishes to Robert and me. There would be no chance of him unloading on me again – his pride would see to that. He'd locked it solid by declaring I'd made a good choice in Robert as a future husband and not him.

But, what he didn't realize was I'd never understood that I even had a choice. Drake was my friend – so was Robert. Did I love either enough to commit my life and swear my vows before God and man?

I dried my tears on a nearby towel and made my way slowly to the buggy. The horse seemed to sense my mood for she cantered along at an easy pace all the way to town. Upon arrival, the buildings now looming before me shocked me back to reality. The journey here had seemed to take but a moment of time.

Robert rushed in a few minutes after I'd settled at a table inside the diner. He remained standing and swallowed hard to catch his breath.

"I'm sorry Clare, but I can't stay. Mrs. Ainsley is about to deliver baby number one and is scared something will go wrong."

"What of Stacy, the new mid-wife? Can she not go?" I asked.

"She's new. Folks are going to have to get used to her being around. Besides, she'd never find them tucked away in the hills like they are."

"Well then, you best hurry, Robert. We don't want the new mother to stress and cause harm to herself or the baby," I said.

"Thank you for understanding. You will make a great wife," he added as he fled from the room. Not even a pat on the hand this time. Suppose this was a public place and some folks may not have heard the news of our courtship yet. Seemed such a fuss for people of our age. Better just get it over with. Like Agnes and Francine had done. They never waited for spring. They were eager brides and couldn't wait to keep house for their Montanan men. Agnes – yes, I'd grab a light lunch, then go for a visit. I recovered from the doctor's departure and eagerly anticipated seeing my friend.

Fifteen minutes later, I walked into the sunshine, in time to view the doctor's buggy speed up as he made haste to leave town. Beside him, Stacy sat tall and erect, a picture of efficiency, but her face beamed and her laugh carried all the way back to me, standing in their dust. I sighed and hurried toward the Mercantile nearly tripping over a parade of ladies heading out.

"Clare," Agnes said. "Fancy seeing you in town. Last I heard you were holed up doing enough preserves to feed the whole ranch."

I laughed. "Yes, I have, but thought I'd take a break and come to town to visit you."

"Well, your timing is perfect. May I introduce Mary, my

cook from Boston and Jillian who will tend to some of my domestic requirements? They both agreed to come and work for me part time so I could continue to help Stanley in the store and not starve him to death in doing so."

"You are excellent with the customers. The whole county is tickled for you to join your husband in running the business," I said.

"And besides my own affairs that I have to stay on top of in Boston. Although young Todd at the bank is an enormous help to me in that area, the bookkeeping does take time."

"In your new office, " I said, excitement touching every word.

"Yes! I am on my way home now to give these ladies a tour. Oh Clare, the workers have done a first-class job and I brought all my favorite things from Haverston. I'm as thrilled as a fresh young bride."

"I can see that." I turned my attention to the two ladies standing quietly off to the side. "Ladies, it is so wonderful to meet you. Are you enjoying Aspen Glen?"

"We've been staying with Maggie at the boarding house until our rooms were completed. But I can tell you, I am relieved to move into a permanent spot tomorrow and finally unpack all my things."

"Likewise," said Jillian. "So far it's been like a holiday. We've been out and about and meeting new people from the church. "Tis a fine town and I will be very happy to live here the rest of my life."

Agnes hugged her. "I am so happy to hear that, Jillian. But, I don't want you to think you are strapped to my side. I want you to have a life of your own. Meeting mine and Stanley's household needs will not take all your time and you must not waste your dressmaking skills." She looked toward me. "Jillian creates great styles with her needle, and I am certain once her dresses appear hanging in the Mercantile and people get to know her, she will have no end of orders."

"Perhaps, Jillian, you can open a shop of your own someday. You have no competition thus far in Aspen Glen," I said.

Jillian caught her breath. "Do you think that might be possible, Ma'am," she was addressing Agnes now.

"Everything is possible in the West," Agnes laughed. "Just look at all of us Easterners taking up residence here."

"Look out, Montana," Mary said, and we all laughed.

"And just look at our Mary. She can make sand taste good. Already has Abigail at the Diner ordering her sweet treats. The Diner is so busy these days and she claims that she enjoys cooking and not baking. Mary is a perfect fit!"

"Looks like life is all unfolding as it should," I said.

Agnes scooped her arm through mine. "Why yes, I hear news of you and the Doctor. Pray tell me the grapevine is not spewing lies?"

I grinned, but from her raised eyebrows I knew the smile never reached my eyes. What was the matter with me? Everyone else appeared to be moving on and all I wanted to do was to stay stuck in my routine with Patrick and Ruth Ellen – even when I realized that was not the healthiest prospect for my son's family.

Agnes patted my arm. "We'll talk later, dear." She called out to the others. "Shall we be off? I am anxious to show you all our home. I decided to name it FischerCrest."

"You've named yer home, Ma'am?" Jillian asked. "Don't see that to be the norm in these parts."

"Phooey! Whoever said I was cookie-cutter normal?"

We all giggled like a bunch of schoolgirls let loose, and hurried down the boardwalk toward the edge of town where Stanley and Agnes Fischer now resided, soon to be joined by the two hired ladies.

An hour later, Jillian and Mary left FischerCrest excited to return at once to the boarding house and begin packing.

"Agnes, you have a fine home. The best in the whole territory, I'm sure, besides PJ's, of course. But the homestead at Jones Star Ranch is a relaxed comfortable style, whereas yours is as classy as you are."

"Why thank you. I tried to add homey touches for Stanley. At times he finds all my stuff overwhelming, but the man claims to be happy as long as I'm happy. To be honest, I'd live with him in one of those shoddy looking shacks I see scattered throughout the countryside. I love that man more than words can say."

"How did you know he was the one to replace your first husband, Carl?" I asked.

"Can't live without the man breathing down my neck." Agnes laughed. Even with our enormous chasm of differences, neither of us could go back to the way it was before we met. We just know deep down that we were meant to be together. Besides, he makes me feel like a young woman again. Who could have ever guessed second love to be so perfect?"

"I am delighted for you, Agnes. And Francine, how is she settling in at the Jamieson ranch?" I asked.

"She was a bit fearful of the whole thing at first, but at the same time, more sure about it than anything in her entire life. And my ex-daughter-in-law is rising to the role of motherhood quite efficiently and Daniel's children both love her to near smothering most days." Agnes grinned. "Glad to say, his old place is getting a much-needed facelift, whether Daniel likes it or not – although Francine is incorporating the changes more slowly than I am. She wants to give her new family a chance to get used to having a wealthy wife and mother without jamming it down their throats straight off."

"Sounds like everyone is adjusting to their new lives and roles. God has blessed us all exceedingly," I said.

My lips trembled and I looked away, but not before the keen eye of the elderly lady caught my change of tone.

"All of us, dear? Do you feel blessed to become Mrs. Clare Palatsie?" Agnes asked.

I turned back toward my friend and sighed. "Palatsie doesn't roll off my lips as easily as Fischer does yours," I said.

"Names are not what I meant," Agnes said.

"I know, but hard as I try, I can't muster up the same assurance as you and Francine appear to have. I'm content to serve my son and his family for the rest of my life. Why do men have to complicate that?"

"Men? Now that sounds interesting? Let me pour us another bit of tea." Agnes lifted the silver pot and filled our cups to the brim.

"I should have said man. Slip of the tongue," I said.

"Too late. The cat is out of the bag. Tell all and I promise none of it will hit the grapevine." She lifted her cup to her lips and raised her eyebrows urging me to continue. "I'm waiting, dear."

"Agnes, Robert is the only honorable choice of husband. He cares for me, and bends over backwards to please me. He even brought me flowers - what more does a woman need?" I laughed attempting to keep of the conversation light.

"Love – spine tingling, joyous spontaneous love. That's what this old woman needs and wants. Wouldn't settle for anything less." Agnes placed her cup firmly in the saucer and penetrated my evasive eyes. "Don't try to hide from me. Others have attempted it in vain."

"When you were all in Boston, I felt overwhelmed with all the harvest ripening, and PJ's cook, Drake, came alongside to help. We worked many hours in the kitchen putting preserves away for the winter."

"Mm... And perhaps you were a tad lonely with everyone

gone?" Agnes asked.

I smiled. "He did fill that void as well – whittling away the long hours and keeping the ghosts away."

"I don't believe I've met the man. Is he nice? A silly question – of course, he's nice. I see a glow in those betraying cheeks of yours."

"Nice and marriage material is not the same thing, Agnes."

"Oh? Enlighten me," she said as she winked mischievously.

"My love life is not a game, Agnes. It distresses me and I just want to run and hide in my room till the world stops spinning."

"Why do you suspect that this Drake is not the marrying kind?" Agnes asked.

"Oh he has nothing against marriage – just not to me. Simply put, he bore his heart, I broke it, and now he won't give me the time of day. Then to top it off, Robert comes calling, asks to court me and I accept – God knows why."

"Rebound? You shun the man you want and take the man you don't. With all the matchmaking your son did, PJ must be thrilled that the doctor will be joining the Jones clan."

She'd thrown out the bait and was dragging the line in. Successful catch. This woman was clever and I'd been hooked.

"PJ and Ruth Ellen are ecstatic. A doctor is a worthwhile catch for any woman." My rushed words sounded almost apologetic, and I felt a heat flush rise from behind my neck.

"Only if she loves him."

"I respect him, admire him, appreciate his kindness, enjoy his company, I really do." The continued rush of words did nothing to convince Agnes. She raised her eyebrows.

"He sounds like a wonderful friend."

"The concept of a man friend is not all it's cracked out to be," I said.

"It is when you leave it there and don't attempt to conjure up the earth-shattering tingles that don't exist," she said.

"How would I know about tingles? The man has never once kissed me. He came close at the hospital, but then backed off and I certainly didn't feel tingles anticipating it, just a curiosity of sorts."

"Talk it, woman. You may figure this out yet." Agnes slurped the last of her tea and replaced the cup to its saucer.

"It's not that simple. How can I take back Robert's proposal without hurting the man? I won't do it Agnes, even if I regret it my entire life. The doctor needs someone to care for him. He gives to everyone else so selflessly, the least I can do is..."

"Become a martyr!" Agnes interrupted. "Do you really think that's what the doctor wants? He's survived being a bachelor a long time before you came to Aspen Glen."

"He must want a wife now or he wouldn't have asked to court me," I said.

"You, my dearest Clare, have a lot of soul searching to do. And you need to promise me you will not say your vows until clarity returns to your mind."

"Clarity? Yes, that is sadly lacking these days," I said.

"Good, at least we are agreed on that," Agnes said. "Now, if you are not going to share the nitty-gritty details about your Drake with me, I must bid you good-day and return to the store. The place is hopping with folks filling their pantries and buying ingredients for the church picnic. You are coming, aren't you, Clare?"

"Of course. I'm in charge of the children's activities, although I'm uncertain as to why the new school teacher didn't volunteer. It would have provided an opportunity to get to know her future students."

"Maybe she didn't want to tackle it alone. Most likely

she'll cozy up and help you with the youngsters come Sunday," Agnes said.

"Perhaps she is shy. I haven't met her yet."

"Chelan – shy? I dare say not. You've heard our Gerald is interested in the spirited filly, right?"

"I'm afraid I've been out of the loop. So much family news happened while everyone was in Boston, and then I was gone from Aspen Glen when you all returned." I smiled. "Yes, I believe Sunday will be a good catch up day for me."

Not only did I feel on the outside looking in, but deep down I suspected it was not simply my lack of knowing the going's on of the people around me but my dilemma over my new role in this community. People would have high expectations from the doctor's wife. I wondered if I would measure up or if they would see clear through me the same as Agnes had.

Chapter 6

Sunday morning rolled around and the Jones household bustled with activity. "Do you have the custard pie, Ma," Ruth Ellen asked. "It's Granny's favorite, although I don't know why I care to spoil her anymore. She has her own cook and can order up all the custard pie she wants."

I saw her eyes twinkle the way it does when she comes up with a new idea. She shimmied up next to her husband.

"PJ. I have an idea kicking around in my mind. Do you want to hear it?" she asked.

"Do I have a choice?"

She clicked her tongue and pretended to be annoyed. "With your Ma thinking of leaving us to set up housekeeping with Doctor Palatsie, do you suppose we might hire a cook to help me around the kitchen here?"

"A cook? Whatever happened? You used to like to cook." Patrick looked confused.

"I do, but I like horses and babies better. Besides, I have all my inheritance money sitting in the bank doing nothing. I can afford a cook. It won't cost the ranch a single penny."

"Where would she live? I don't want a stranger under our roof."

"Well, maybe one of the wives of your workers in the cabins nearby is looking for a bit of extra cash. She could just prepare it for us. I can heat it and get it on the table. I'm not an invalid."

Patrick looked my way, thunderstruck, and I chuckled at his expression. "You started this whole thing with Robert and me. It's your fault I'm leaving."

"I didn't tell you to go. You can change your mind," he said.

My mind slipped down that dangerous path of choices. Could it be as easy as that? I dismissed it. What was done was done. "PJ, you wouldn't want me to break Robert's heart now, would you? It must have took a lot of courage for him to come asking to court me."

His eyebrows lifted and his mouth pressed tight before he spoke. "Really? Drama was never your forte, Ma."

"But it is Ruth Ellen's. How can you ignore those puppy dog eyes?"

"A cook! I already pay one cook at the mess hall. Why don't we just eat there?"

"What a grand idea!" Ruth Ellen squealed.

"I was kidding. I won't have my family sitting amongst the hired hands listening to their cowboy talk."

"True. But I can pick it up from Cook before I head home," said Ruth Ellen.

"And where will the baby be all this time – in the barn?" PJ sighed. "Let's agree to put this discussion on hold, Ruth Ellen. Ma is here until after the baby is born and things may look a lot different then. Perhaps your priorities will change."

"Don't count on it," she yelled from inside the pantry. "Hey, I found the pie. Are we almost ready to go? I'm so eager to meet the new preacher."

"Is that what this is all about? I never saw you so agitated and feather-brained," said Patrick.

"Feather-brained! I don't think that is a compliment, sir."

Wisely, Patrick avoided that comment. "Are we ready, ladies? Clock's ticking and we don't want to be late, right, Ruth Ellen?"

"Right," she said as she hurried out the door. "I'll put this in the picnic box. I am so excited I could scream into the wind."

"Go ahead," called Patrick. "Give us a break." He looked my way and shook his head. "Do all expectant women get this crazy?"

"Everyone is different. But most men will agree that patience is the key to holding it together till the baby comes, and sometimes even afterwards." I laughed and bounced out the door ahead of him.

You could barely see the doors of the church for the teams of wagons pulling up to park. The whole territory must be gathering for this event. Out of the corner of my eye I noticed familiar faces.

"Look PJ, it's the Wright family! Came all the way from Stanton to worship with us this morning," I said.

"Probably wants to know when the new preacher will be holding services in their valley, or if he'll decide to live there like Reverend Tully," Patrick suggested. "Understand the house sits empty."

"Heaven forbid!" said Ruth Ellen. "That place needs to be demolished."

I laughed. "Agreed, but the community must be feeling the loss of Reverend Tully. Nice to have a man-of-the-cloth nearby."

"I'm told the Tully's have lived in Stanton, in that same

house, for many generations," Ruth Ellen said. "I am sorry we didn't get a chance to say goodbye. But he is in heaven, so we will meet again, some day."

"That knowledge helps, but doesn't make the parting of this life any easier for those of us left behind," Patrick said.

We all agreed as Mr. Wright waved at us. We stepped clear of the wagon and Patrick thrust his hand out in greeting. "Mr. Wright. Pleased to see y'all on this grand morning."

"The name's John, and this here is my wife, Nelly." As the children lined up he named them one after another. I recognized the one he called Trish as the young girl who often brought me food.

"So nice to see you again, Trish. I never had a chance to thank you for the many trips you made to the outbuilding with food. You were a blessing to the doctor and me."

"My pleasure, Ma'am," she said as she edged closer in behind her mother. She was shy but I'd pull that out of her when we gathered for games with the other children this afternoon.

"This is my wife, Ruth Ellen," Patrick introduced. He gathered her into the circle with his arm. "These are the kind folks who offered shelter and food to Ma and Doctor Palatsie while they worked at the hospital in Stanton."

Ruth Ellen stepped forward and swept the woman into her arms. "We are so thankful for your kindness. Ma's welfare is very important to us."

The woman seemed surprised at Ruth Ellen's unreserved show of affection but closed her eyes for the brief seconds of the encounter as if to savor such familiarity. The community of Stanton was an extremely reserved bunch and held one another at a safe distance. Of course, Ruth Ellen never even noticed the woman's awkwardness. My daughter-in-law was the most forthcoming, gracious woman the dear Lord put on this earth.

"You must sit with us at lunch and tell us of the rebuilding of lives in Stanton after such a great loss. We here choose to celebrate the positive aspect rather than wither away in the enemy's pit of negativity – and there is plenty of that to be found, I'm sure." She held the woman at arms length. "You will join us, won't you?"

The woman smiled. No one could resist Ruth Ellen's enthusiasm and positive outlook for long. "That would be nice." She glanced at her husband and when he nodded his approval she said, "thank you for the invitation."

"Patrick will show your husband where to put the food. Let's head inside and grab a seat. Gracious me, you will need an entire pew just for your family. I can't wait for the Jones' to fill an entire pew. What do you think about that, PJ?" She winked his way and was gone, ushering the family toward the new church building. I followed beside the young girl, Trish.

"Do you like games?" I asked.

"Don't have much time fer it at home. Chores keep me busy, and I'm studying real hard to be a teacher."

"That is a noble profession and much needed in the West. But at the same time, you will need to know how to play and interact with your students. So, if I were you, I'd indulge in some fun from time to time."

Her face lit up. "I reckon yer right, Ma'am.

"Of course, I am. You will meet Aspen Glen's new teacher today. This is her first posting so she may be a bit nervous – greeting all the new faces."

"A real teacher! One of the mothers comes in town fer our book learnin' a couple times a week. Leaves a lot to do fer homework but I think it will make me stronger in the end."

"Definitely more disciplined," I agreed. I pointed to the third row from the front. "Looks like your mother found a pew for you all to sit together. We will be right behind you. A brand new preacher can sometimes be a bit scary, but rest assured, the board interviewed several before landing on this one."

"He looks mighty young, don't he, Ma'am?" Trish asked.

I smiled. "Yes, he does. But perhaps he's had his nose buried in the Good Book since he was in diapers and will inspire even us older folks."

"I do hope so. Folks need to hear some words of life. Too much death on everyone's mind back home," she said.

"You are a wise young girl whom I believe will touch many lives in your teaching future. Stay to the mark and you'll always overcome," I said.

She hurried to the front and took her place with the row of children. I smiled and wondered if Ruth Ellen would be satisfied with such an achievement as that – a row of Jones children. My grandchildren. My heart swelled with pride and I startled when someone touched my elbow.

"Good morning, Clare."

"Ah, Robert, you caught me musing again."

"Will you do the honor of sitting with me?"

I stammered. "Can you squeeze in with us? I promised the young Trish that I'd be right behind her today."

"As you wish. I'm sure my spot will be eagerly snatched up. Quite a crowd gathering for the first Sunday of the new season."

"Not to mention the new minister. Have you met him yet, Robert?"

"Yes, and I'm certain you will be pleased – a godly man with wisdom beyond his years. Spouts it through the innocence of youth. A delightful combination and a welcome addition to our growing community."

A broad smile covered my face. "Yes indeed. God is good to supply the need when we pray."

It was during the third song of the morning worship that I sensed the eyes on me. I glanced around me and stopped at the disconcerting gaze of the usually joyous Stacy Trop. I smiled as our eyes met and she cracked her lips upward in polite response. Now what had I done to offend her? Perhaps she was put out at the mess I'd left for her at the hospital. After my two days absentee while laid sick in bed, the hospital room was probably a smelly shambles when she arrived to take my place amongst the sick. Stacy turned her attention to the front and opened her mouth to sing. Our scrutiny lasted only an instant, and I wondered if I'd imagined the whole silent encounter with the woman. I felt Robert stir beside me and looked his way. He scrutinized me with the detail of a fine-toothed comb. I squirmed and looked away. I felt his fingers touch mine, but it felt more like an apology rather than an intimate gesture. I ignored it, and with all that was left of my poise, transferred my hand to grip the pew in front of me.

I slipped from the service during the final song to join the committee members. People would be hungry after such a great sermon – food for the soul and now food for the stomach.

I felt him before I actually saw him, and when I turned, we collided. The dish of potato salad teetered in my shaky hands.

"Oh, goodness, I didn't see you." I stammered; suddenly my tongue stuck on the roof of my mouth. His nearness sent my senses swirling and I felt the burning rush of red flow into my cheeks.

"Can I help carry some of the food to the serve yerself table?" Drake asked with a tantalizing smile on his face. Was he poking fun at me?

I bit my lip. In straightening my posture, my eyes drew parallel to his and it was all I do to breathe. "Certainly. All help is appreciated."

"I'll remember that," he said in that playful teasing voice that always drew me into fun mode.

My lower lip received a second bite, and his eyes glued

me to the spot. This would never do. I shook free of his hold on me. "We need to hurry. The parishioners will be gathering soon and expect to be fed."

I skirted around his solid frame and escaped from the schoolhouse where we'd stored the mountains of food. I sucked in the fresh air outside, relieved to have put space between us, and hurried toward the table. Drake appeared to be everywhere, bringing two rounds of food to the table to my one. I raced to keep up and with each trip, found myself relaxing. This was our game and he knew it well. What was he up to? Flirting with the doctor's fiancée? I should be ashamed – yet I wasn't. A minute of fun wouldn't hurt anyone – or so I thought.

On my last trip to the table I sensed another set of eyes. It was Julia Thip, the queen of the town grapevine, on the lookout for new tidbits of gossip to fill her conversation this afternoon. I supposed Drake and I would qualify for her yack-trap, for she stood with her arms crossed staring at our competitive race to the finish line. Drake pushed in behind me and threw down his plate of sliced meat. He followed my gaze and nudged me.

"Did I get ya in trouble?" he asked.

"Probably, but it's not all your fault. I'm a big girl and didn't have to fall prey to your challenge."

"Challenge? Is that what we're calling it?" he asked. I turned to face him and abruptly felt the heat move up the back of my neck. "You're face is flushed, Mrs. Jones."

"Don't flatter yourself. It's all the rushing back and forth that's making me hot."

"Mm… I reckon I deserve that."

"You certainly do. You made your position to me quite clear and I'm moving on as you suggested. So you tell me – is this fair what you're doing here today?"

"Flirting with a woman betrothed to another? Unheard of and definitely a prime target for the gossipers of Aspen Glen."

Drake took off his hat and bowed slightly. "I apologize and will cause you no further grief."

I grabbed his hand as he turned to leave. "Drake, we need to talk. We are too old to play games that will affect others."

"Ya mean the doctor? No, Clare, he is still the best choice. Good day to ya."

And then he was gone. He was like a ghost, here one minute and gone the next. However, was I to survive this teeter-totter of emotions that caused such upheaval inside my body? I blinked a tear away that searched to find a way of escape to the outside. Its release would not find favor with this crowd, and I once again attempted to straighten my form and behave in a way that suited my age and station.

It was then I noticed Robert coming around the corner. What had I done to the poor man? The gossip-vine would whittle us down to pint-size before the day was over. Before he'd gone a few steps, Stacy barricaded his path. I could only see the outline of her back, but Robert's face was in full view. His expression changed every minute, it seemed, from serious to light-hearted, and all reactions in-between. I wondered the last time our conversations had caused such life to define his features. Once again the thought plagued my confusion – why me? Why did the doctor ask to court me immediately after this joyful woman, who obviously amused him, entered his life?

Robert and I dined under the tree surrounded by family and friends. To avoid the sudden silence that seemed to haunt my withdrawn fiancé, I occupied my time in conversation with Trish. The young girl was interesting and full of hope for the future and unbeknown to her, I fed off her spirit. As we cleaned up the mess we'd left on the blanket, Stacy hurried over.

"Doctor Palatise," she called slightly out of breath. "A man has ridden in and is looking for you. Seems his boy fell from a high branch on a tree and is lyin' unconscious in the back of his wagon. I'll run and set up the room in our office. Please hurry." She glanced sideways at me and added, "Sorry to steal yer man, Ma'am."

She did not look the least bit sorry but I supposed I would have to get used to Robert being called away. Emergencies would interrupt many moments of my future.

"Duty calls, Mrs. Trop. I have no problem with that." I smiled at Robert. "You did warn me that trees and boys spoiled most of your picnic days."

Robert grinned, and his face screamed the apology he did not put into words.

I felt a weight lift from my shoulders as I watched the two of them dash toward the main street. Was that normal? My mind went back to the tingling I'd felt at Drake's nearness and wondered if that was the reaction that Agnes had hinted at when we'd talked in her kitchen the other day. Minus the guilt, tingles would be a welcome distraction right now. I allowed myself to scan the area and before too long spotted Drake talking with others of Patrick's employ.

"PJ, that was kind of you to give your men time off to join us today," I said as he passed by on way to the wagon to unload his arms laden with soiled dishes and leftovers.

"My men know any of them are free to worship on any given Sunday. I'll not hinder the Lord should he be drawing them to the altar. Food was the big draw today, but the boys heard the Word spoken and that's a dance card the Holy Spirit can work with all week long."

"Yes, I believe the new preacher was received well. Lots of agreeable conversation flowing free about him."

Patrick snickered. "Some tighter circles here today could have used a touch of virtuous conversation."

Heat began to rise into my face, and Patrick bellowed louder. "I see the grapevine finally got it right. So, what's up with you and Drake? I recall you saying you'd done some preserving together while I was gone. Something more you're not telling me?" he asked with a hint of mischief brewing in his eyes.

"PJ, this is not the time or the place. I have games ready to play with the children. Do you think the new schoolteacher will come help? I don't know her so didn't feel right in asking."

"She's the one dragging Gerald around by her baby finger, making him introduce her to every available bachelor in town. Don't think he's happy about that, but he does appear to be smitten with the gal."

"Well, give it no mind if she's busy getting acquainted. But, I do hope she speaks to some of the families. I know many ladies were excited to meet up with her. I wouldn't want town folk to think she is simply in Aspen Glen to find a man."

"I believe I may suggest it to her. I saw a few disapproving glances cast her way from a few of the mothers," said Patrick.

"Drop a hint about the children's events as well. She should focus. School is about to start up and it would benefit both her and the students to have a bit of fun together before she saddles them with book learning." I started to walk away. "Best get the games set up before I lose them all to tree climbing. Robert doesn't need any more patients to ruin his day, now does he?"

I hurried to the wagon and grabbed the bag I'd prepared and then departed for a nearby field. I pounded a post with a colourful picture nailed on it into the ground.

"All children welcome," a voice sounded behind me. I spun around and nearly toppled into Drake's arms. He held my surprised gaze. "Does that include me? Am I welcome?"

"Drake," I gasped, slightly out of breath from his nearness.

"Having trouble concentrating?"

"You do not play fair, sir."

"I like to live on the wild side, How 'bout you?"

"I hate unpredictability."

"Your responses to my meddlin' beg to differ. And I recall a certain woman who doused me in flour and left me white and hopeless to follow her predictable life to Stanton."

"Is that the way you see it?"

"Is there another way? Do you even know what you want in a man?"

"As a matter fact – no! Is that what you want to hear? I know nothing about men except they confuse me and distract me from things that matter."

He raised his eyebrow and let me rant. "Such as children's events? I'd love to help. Been a while since I mixed with the youngsters but I think I'd like to try again."

I remembered the story of him losing his son and my compassion won over. "Drake, do you miss your son horribly?"

"He'd be a full grown man now. But we used to fish and hunt. Taught him to play ball – he had a strong arm on him." His thoughts seemed to wander and I mellowed as I watched his expression soften and genuine laugh lines infiltrate his face.

I blurted the response from my heart and dared the gossipers to have their way with us.

"I would love your help, Drake. Organizing and running games at a picnic is a task not many are willing to help with."

"Children can be exhausting when you're not used to them."

"And that would be us, right?" I asked.

He laughed and I could not stop my heart from soaring. "But we're fresh meat for them to carve up. Let's take a go at it, girl."

I drew strength from his enthusiasm and joined in his merriment, casting all notions to the wind of the manner in which a woman slated to be married to the prestigious doctor should behave. In Drake's presence, the air somehow changed, freshening into a sweet smell of fall harvest. The scent of late-blooming flowers caressed my nostrils while a gentle breeze cooled the heated blush from my face. Once again, it was just Drake and I, lost in our own world, creating a brand new recipe flavor to entice our senses.

I wondered briefly how this day would all be served up in the end, but quickly dismissed the temptation to analyze and dampen the mood. Tomorrow would look after itself.

Twenty minutes later I scurried closer to the crowd, cleared my voice, and made the announcement. Calling all children! Fun and games are awaiting you in yonder field."

I was not prepared for the exodus of little bodies that blazed past me. I felt their excitement and hurried to catch up. Drake was already giving instructions and handing out burlap sacks for the first race. I moved to the finish line and signaled for him to start the competition. Standing ankle deep in grass, I felt momentum seep into my predictable bones and giggled like a schoolgirl as Drake shouted, ready, set, go; and when the last duo crossed the chalk line in the grass, I squealed and grabbed the arms of the winning team and thrust them into the air declaring the first place winners!

I scribbled their names into the book I carried and when finished, glanced up to see Gerald leading the new teacher, Chelan, our way. Her presence in the children's area excited me. It felt good to be alive and enjoying the afternoon with God's people, both young and old, in Aspen Glen, Montana.

Although the young teacher stayed fixed on the sidelines, over the next hour the children toddled her way, one by one, and introduced themselves. She bent low to speak to each one, eye to eye, and her smile was warm and sincere. She'd do all right in the classroom. It appeared she held a special place for children close to her heart and did not for one moment treat them as carelessly as the men that she'd flirted with earlier at the picnic. I hoped
that the concerned mothers were watching this new bond developing between their children and the new teacher.

Drake was attempting to get my attention. "Mrs. Jones," he called rather loudly. When I caught his eye he smiled accusingly, knowing that I was musing once again over matters of the heart. I swore that man could read my thoughts.

"Yes, Mr..." Phooey! I couldn't remember his last name. "Drake," I emphasized instead and watched the busy bees gathering close in huddle to discuss my latest no-no of the day.

When we met up, Drake said, "By the way, the last name is Whitfield – just in case you're testing how it sounds next to Clare." He grinned and I slapped him.

"Don't cross the line with a woman promised to another man." Yet, somehow his idea touched a funny bone and I couldn't help but do as he suggested. *Clare Whitfield*, I mused.

He laughed outright as he handed me the passing-stick. "Just what I thought. Sounds good, eh?"

I turned quickly so he could not see me turn a bright crimson. "The game, sir. I'll run to the first flag and trust that you can drag your sorry butt close enough to relieve me of the stick. It's hard to believe the children can't follow these simple instructions."

"Maybe they just want to see us run," he suggested.

"I'm too old for this," I said.

"Thankfully, we made the distance between flags short. Think team red and let's win this one together."

I could have said we already won by the color that refused to leave my face but I figured that jest had been carried far enough. I placed two of the older children at the last two flags and pushed a dramatic Drake to the second one. Team red was in position. Gerald volunteered to do the countdown and at the word, go, I sprinted and ran as fast as my legs would carry me to flag one. I lifted the flag high in the air and never let up the pace. Drake fell in beside me and grabbed the stick from my hand before we reached the allotted distance to pass. I stopped and he raced on. I watched as Drake sped toward the next eager teammate who was jumping up and down enthusiastically. Drake's muscles flexed as he moved in a steady, but fast rhythm, like music blowing in the wind. I fanned myself, hoping the blast of heat that invaded me now was simply the result of my being winded.

At the finish line the last child in our foursome, held the stick high and shouted. "And that's how it's done, folks."

Everyone laughed and new teams of four took their positions as we wearily headed back to ours to complete the race all over again. Our red team came in third the second time we raced, and we all cheered for the winners – a yellow team of boys who looked athletic enough to run a mile and not be winded.

I returned to the starting line and collapsed. Patrick joined me laughing. "Now there's a happy face if I ever saw one."

"The children are having such fun. I'm so glad I volunteered for this job, although I must admit I'm relieved that the next event is a quiet bean-bag toss."

"I'll do it if you like, Mrs. Jones," said a voice from behind. "Give you a chance to catch your breath."

I looked as Chelan loomed in front of me. She was one tall girl. "That would be appreciated. Thank you, Chelan."

"My pleasure. The young ones are a delightful bunch, aren't they? Much more respectful than the lot in Boston. You know, I only lasted two days teaching in a Girl's Academy, but please, but don't tell anyone. I did not include that work venture in my letter of application to teach in Aspen Glen. I figured a greenhorn sounded better than a failure."

"Don't despair. You are off to a marvelous start. First day in the classroom will be much easier now that you've broken the ice with the children on the play field."

"I think so too. I'll be off then. Over there, right?" she pointed.

Patrick stood and offered his arm to Chelan. "Let me escort you while the losers rest from their efforts."

It was only then I noticed Drake standing off to the side. I did not miss the stern look my son cast his way. They'd had words, and I concluded I was about to be enlightened.

Chapter 7

"What was that look for?' I asked Drake.

He proceeded to plunk himself in the grass beside me. "Just looking out fer his Ma. Told PJ he might have been keener when the good doctor came callin'."

"You did, did you? And how did that reprimand go for you?" I asked.

"Got me an audience with yer son and my boss, which made the confrontation a bit touchy."

"You were seeking an audience with my son? Whatever for?"

"Ya can be rather dense when you set yer mind to it," he said with playful annoyance in his tone.

"Now that's the way to compliment a lady," I said, not the least bit put out by his remark.

"Most ladies would have gotten the hint by now," he said.

"Maybe I'm not looking for hints since I appear to be sworn to another."

"Ya ain't married to the bloke yet. Stop using it as an excuse." He sobered. "Thing is, I'm interested in explorin' to see if we have a chance at somethin' beyond friendship – if'n ya know what I mean." I held back the smile as I listened to his awkward appeal. "I was stupid and premature to send you packin' at the first sign of attraction between us. Not sure why I did - just did."

I wanted to treat his honesty with respect so I followed suit. "You confuse me and I hate being confused. I can't deal with that in a man again."

"So ya grabbed the easy route as soon as it was presented to ya - a dutiful wife waiting at home for her husband to finish up with his never-ending emergencies." He was winding up now. "And ya said yes to his proposition so quick I didn't have time to apologize and backtrack. Truth is woman, I fell in love with ya while laying on the floor, flour all over our bodies and panting from all the chaos we'd created with our funnin'."

I finished for him. "Then Robert showed up, and you felt rejected when I left you to go with him to Stanton."

"Suppose I did. While ya was gone I heard all the before-stories about you two, forever goin' in circles but not committin' to anythin' permanent like. PJ was rootin' for the union so I decided to back off. Although, I couldn't resist the trip to Stanton when I heard you was sickly. That backfired too."

"So why now?" I asked.

"PJ told me if I didn't get my act together you'd go off and marry a man ya didn't love."

"My son told you that?"

"Gave his blessing, sort'a, but warned I'd better not mess ya up or he'd come chasin' after me with a snake whip."

"My son would not whip you," I said.

"I know that, but the threat woke me from my snoozin'."

"So what do you think I should do? Give up on a sure thing and throw my lot in with you on a chance?" I pressed my lips together to hold back the grin. I did not want him to suspect

I was pulling his leg, for I knew given half a chance I would fall madly in love with this man.

He missed the cue and quickly jumped to his feet. "That'd be yer call. Won't be beggin' ya again. Ya know where to find me." He tipped his hat and stalked off toward a string of horses tied to a tree. I let him go. At the moment I was not free to respond and new agony set into my heart. Robert did not deserve this betrayal.

It was well into late afternoon before the families started pulling out. I hugged the Wright's and gave Trish one last word of encouragement.

"If you need any extra help with your schoolwork, ask your Pa to bring you over, or send word and I'll come get you. I'm sure our new teacher here will offer help to a serious minded student. I expect you to graduate and become the best teacher Montana has ever had."

"Thank you, Ma'am. Had a great day, eatin' and playin' games. And I hope the new preacher decides to live in Stanton like the old one. People in the next valley need all the hope a man of God can give 'em."

"I heard today that he plans to come to Stanton, at least temporarily. We'll have to see what the future holds," I said.

I watched the Wright family pull out onto the road and glanced nervously toward the doctor's office. The wagon that had brought in the injured boy was still parked outside. Patrick and Ruth Ellen were busy talking with neighbors. I caught my son's attention and pointed toward the middle of town. He understood the message and waved me on.

I strolled toward my destination, fear badgering every step. My eyes stayed glued to the medical building so as not to become distracted. A visit to the general store would be preferred over my encounter with Robert. *Coward*, I chided myself and forced my feet to keep moving. Before opening the door, I plastered on my biggest smile and turned the knob.

Inside the main room a lone man paced the floor. "How is your son doing?" I asked.

"Doc is not givin' him much hope. Says he won't wake up." A sudden thought came to the man and he brightened. "Same thing happened to yer Ruthie, right? Got hit on the head real bad. She woke up and is walkin' round today. Could happen that way with my boy."

"It certainly could. All injuries are different, sir, but there always remains hope."

"The Good Lord got him a bunch of young'uns up in heaven but my wife and me, we only got one boy," he said as if that reasoning would sway the hand of God.

"Would you like me to pray with you?" I asked.

"Not a man to bend my knee, Ma'am, but ya could try if ya like."

I made the prayer simple so as not to scare off the father's first attempt at praying. "Lord, we know that you loved our children long before we ever had a chance to hold them in our arms. But hold and cherish them we do, and this young son lies between life and death – you and us. The family you chose to nurture his young life is begging for you to intercede. If it is in your plan to see him full grown, we lift him to you now and ask for a complete healing. Let the miracle bring honor and glory to the name of Jesus, Amen."

I opened my eyes to see the man teary-eyed and staring at me. "Thank ya. Made me feel all warm and fuzzy. Is that a good thing?"

"Our feelings fluctuate minute by minute. But God is compassionate, and when our senses are touched, it is the result of an encounter with him. So yes, I think your warm fuzzies are a good thing." I moved closer, took his hand and led him to a chair. "I'll pour you a cup of coffee. May I sit with you and wait until the

the doctor comes out?"

"That'd be nice, Mrs. Jones." He fidgeted then drew his attention from the closed door where his son lay, and said. "Hear you and the doctor are tying the knot?"

If I was forced to answer that question once more today I felt sure I'd burst. I should have never agreed to marry Robert and now the whole town would know that I led the poor man on. At least, my bearing the blame would save the doctor's reputation and I supposed in the long run that's all that mattered. I could easily hide at the ranch until the gossip died down and a new scandal made its way to the forefront.

"We are courting. Is that the same thing as married?" Perhaps asking a stranger would serve as a means to ease my guilty conscience.

He cast a strange look my way. "I reckon courtin' is a way to tell the other fellas to stand down, that yer taken. But it ain't in stone till the preacher says the words over ya."

"Well, then yes, we are courting – testing the waters." I noticed his confusion and shut my mouth. "Yer coffee is cold. Let me pour another." I sprang to my feet and hurried to the stove.

"It's a might strong, Mrs. Jones, like mud. Maybe ya could stir up a new pot?"

"Of course. Excellent idea. I'll bring one into the doctor as well. He must need some perking-up tending to your son all this time."

"Got the new nurse in there with him. Ya like the woman, Mrs. Jones?"

"I barely know her, but I do appreciate that her skills will help lighten Dr. Palatsie's heavy patient load."

"Do ya think the mid-wife knows a secret way to get my woman's womb more in tune to birthin' babies? Long time between young'uns."

"I think that the Lord needs to help in that department. I

will pray for your wife," I said.

"Appreciate that. Makes her feel right jealous when others spit them babes out as easy as a seed from a grape."

I urged the new pot to brew and felt a flood of relief when I was able to hand him a second cup of coffee. By now, Patrick would be waiting for me, ready to head home and get to his chores. A talk with Robert would have to wait for another day. I'd just slip in a couple of cups and be on my way.

I placed the drinks on a small tray, with sugar and cream, and carried it to the sick room. I tapped lightly and walked in. Robert and Stacy stood silently by the window – so close their bodies touched – but neither seemed to notice or care. They turned abruptly upon my arrival and I saw a tinge of color rush into Robert's face. Stacy remained cool and smiled.

"Fresh coffee! Thank you, Mrs. Jones."

She took the tray and Robert pulled me to the side while she busied with preparing the cup the way she liked it.

"I am so sorry for deserting you at the picnic," he said.

"Nonsense. Would I have the boy die while we ate and visited? You underestimate my compassion for your work, doctor." I called him doctor! How informal was that. He appeared not to pick up on it so I continued. "How is the child?"

"Not good. Done all I can and now it's just a waiting game."

"Do you not think his father might want to be in here sharing the waiting time?" I asked.

"How insensitive of me. Of course, the man must be stir-crazy."

"Can I send him in before I leave? PJ is waiting to go home. You can come calling when you find time to spare. We need to talk," I said.

"Yes, indeed. Planning a special day takes so much time, doesn't it?"

Not exactly what I wanted to discuss. But this was not the time or place to bring up the question of us. "I'll expect you at the ranch then, at your earliest convenience," I said, and turned to go. Was that relief I saw sneaking into his face? Perhaps he dreaded what we'd done worse than I did. I could only hope.

Outside the sick room, I spoke to the father who immediately stood at attention hoping for news. "The doctor says you can come into the room with your coffee and sit with them. They are waiting for him to wake up as well. Remember to draw strength from the fact that we gave his healing over to the Lord. I hope that comforts you no matter what happens."

"Been talkin' to the big man on my own since ya left with the coffee. Not so hard once you set yer mind to it."

I smiled and tried to set the untaught man straight. "God is not a *big man*. He is *God Almighty* and we would do well to keep the two separate in our minds. He promises to be with us in both the good times and the bad." Now was not the time or place for a whole lesson on theology. Soon enough he'd fall in love with the God-Man Jesus if he kept his heart in search mode.

I grabbed hold of his arm and led him to the door. I opened it in time to see Stacy on her tiptoes planting a peck of a kiss on the doctor's cheek, then scurry away. He appeared surprised and stared after her with a confused expression on his face. As for me, the woman's forwardness did not surprise me, or bother me.

The atmosphere changed in a heartbeat. The child stirred and both Robert and the father rushed to his side. I stood back and watched as the boy groaned and reached for his head, now wrapped in a slightly bloody cloth. He then looked at his father and the tears came.

"Oh Pa. I just had the most perfect dream. I didn't want to wake up but then it all faded and I was back in bed lookin' at you."

"How are ya feeling, son?" asked the man.

The boy grinned. "Like climbing another tree."

I smothered a laugh but the doctor let it rip. "We are glad to hear you say that, boy. Well, maybe not your Pa. You gave us all quite a scare."

"No need to be scared when you close your eyes, sir. There be someone waitin' on the other side, and I met him." The child's face shone.

The father turned and walked toward me. He pulled me into a bear hug and whispered in my ear. "I think I met him, too." Stepping back he said, "Thank you, Mrs. Jones. Be seeing you in church come next Sunday. Might keep my boy out of trees for a short spell anyway."

Outside, I noticed PJ parked in front of the Mercantile. Hurrying, I arrived at the door with a heart of thanksgiving and a little short of breath. When I crossed the threshold I noticed Agnes bent over in pain and the family gathered around holding her up. I joined them and her slightly blue face stared at me through wild eyes.

"Agnes, whatever is the matter?" I asked.

"A lot of fuss over nothing. An old lady's body doesn't always digest food like it used to."

"We should take her to the doctor, just to be sure," I suggested.

Stanley agreed. "Exactly what I said."

"He's busy with the boy. I'll not take him from his work," Agnes said.

"It's okay," I said. "The boy just woke up and is in his right mind. A celebration is going on over there."

"That settles it, woman. No more arguing." Stanley took Agnes by the arm and headed toward the door. A train of concerned family followed behind and met the doctor in the main office downing his coffee."

"Robert, Agnes is feeling ill. Would you check it out?"

"Certainly. The boy is still in the room. Come stretch out on this cot in the corner, Agnes, and we'll see what's bothering you."

For a few minutes, PJ, Ruthie and I remained quiet and stood by the stove. Stanley hovered over the cot as the doctor pushed here and there against Agnes' skin and asked his patient questions concerning her day and state of health.

Finally he stood and smiled. "You can all relax. Simply a case of indigestion."

"Just like I said," Agnes said with emphasis.

"Your wife is in excellent health otherwise, Stanley. She may outlive us all."

"Thanks, Doc. I was kinda gettin' used to her bein' around. Not of a mind to lose her to no sickness just yet," Stanley said.

"Not happening on my watch." Agnes swung her legs to the side and stood to her feet. She brushed the wrinkles from her skirt and placed a kiss firmly on Stanley's lips. "I am determined, husband dear, to make every day of your life a little more edgy than the one before. Need to keep you on your toes and your heart beating the love march."

Stanley looked around the room, his cheeks revealing his old shy self. "Behave yourself, woman. Ya make a spectacle of us everywhere we go."

We all laughed and the couple headed for the door. "I'm off for one of those old lady rests. And I will stick to slurping chicken broth until my tummy settles down like you suggested, Doc." She cast a glance behind her. "Don't get old. Some parts are not fun at all." She laughed as Stanley poked her arm and pushed her out the door.

"Those two," Ruth Ellen said. "I can only hope PJ will love me that much when we reach their age."

Patrick responded. "Never fear. It will take two of us to chase all the grandkids around from that string of young'uns you plan on birthing."

"How are you feeling?" Robert asked. "Been so busy, I haven't had a chance to bring Stacy out to examine you. She's helping me, especially with expectant women. It's her expertise, you know."

"Yes, I understand she brought my brother Gerald into the world and helped my mother find him. I will be forever grateful to the woman for bringing us together as family."

Stacy spoke from the doorway. "Ruth Ellen, how nice to see you again. I haven't seen much of you since the trip home on the train."

"Ranch life is extremely busy. We missed you at the picnic this afternoon but we do understand and appreciate the sacrifices doctors and nurses make to keep us all healthy," Ruth Ellen said.

Stacy looked directly at me and said without blinking, "Some people do."

I was taken aback realizing that somehow she was under the impression that I did not support Robert in his work. She had gall – I'd give her that. Then I saw it – the woman was jealous! She wanted Robert for herself – either as a colleague or a husband, or perhaps both, I couldn't be sure. But I was in her way. She had no idea that a simple request from her to move over, and I'd oblige. In that moment, something evil swelled from within and I decided, that for the present, I'd keep the woman guessing.

I walked over to my betrothed and hugged him – the first deliberate one we'd ever shared – but she didn't know that.

"Don't work too late, dear. Save your strength for our next encounter."

I hated myself for the deception but couldn't resist the power I held being Robert's chosen one for the moment. Stacy stomped away and disappeared into the boy's room.

"Speaking of a busy ranch," said Patrick. "We best get headed home. The boys and I have been out playing all day and the chores are piling up."

I led the way out the door with head held high and my insides quivering from my fall from grace.

Chapter 8

The week stretched on. I kept busy with housework and meal preparation but watched every evening for Robert's buggy. The guilt was weighing heavily on me and I needed to put this confrontation behind me. I made no attempt to contact Drake and would not even consider it until after I settled this matter of the heart with Robert. I was not expecting PJ's announcement Thursday night at the dinner table.

"He's gone."

"Who's gone?" Ruth Ellen asked.

"The cook." He looked at me and rephrased it. "Drake is gone."

I sat to attention. "Where?"

"If I knew I'd send the hounds after him." PJ appeared angry and I almost backed down from questioning him further.

I tried a touch of humor. "You didn't whip the man did you?"

"I should have! At least it might make me feel better at him leaving the ranch high and dry without a cook. And leaving you – with whatever it was you two talked about Sunday."

Ruth Ellen attempted to create some form of peace at the table. "PJ, we can help out with the cooking, right Ma. Until you find a replacement."

"I don't want to replace the cook! The boys are spoiled and will string me up if they suspect I'm the cause of his leaving."

"But you're not, Patrick. Drake is a grown man and makes his own choices. Surely your men understand that," I said.

"A hungry cowboy is a hard one to put to work."

I stood to my feet. "Then I will go to the mess hall every day until you figure out what happened to your hired man. I refuse to believe he would just leave you high and dry. He's not that kind of person."

"Have you considered the cook was abducted or seriously injured and lay dying somewhere?" Ruth Ellen suggested.

Patrick calmed down immediately. "I never thought of that. Seems to be lots of second-hand information floating around at the bunkhouse. Not sure anyone saw him leave, but he is gone nonetheless."

"Well, that's it then. You need to investigate further, PJ, and perhaps go for a look-see yourself," I said.

"A look-see? Do you know how far he could have gotten since lunch?"

"He's been gone since lunch? What did the men have for supper?"

"I sent them all to the Diner in town and gave them a bit extra for a drink at the saloon afterward," Patrick said.

"I'm going down there right now and check his pantry. Knowing him, he has something simmering somewhere. His menu was always two days ahead," I said.

"Let me take you," offered Patrick.

"No need. I know a short cut. I'll be there before you can get the horse hooked up to the buggy." I watched his face for some sign of yielding. "I promise to be back by dark. Don't fret. In the meantime, perhaps you two might go for one of your evening horse back rides and take a peek-see?"

I could count on Ruth Ellen to like that idea. "Let's go, PJ. It will help us all sleep better knowing he's not lying out there waiting for some Good Samaritan to ride by."

I grabbed a light shawl off the hook. The evenings were a bit chilly and I wasn't sure the temperature of the deserted mess hall would be any better. I made a right turn at the barn and meandered down a back path toward Drake's place of work. My mind was still spinning from PJ's report. From everything I'd learned about the cook, the whole idea of him abandoning his post at a moment's notice did not make sense.

The door squeaked as I swung it open wide and stepped inside. No noisy men assaulted my ears and no welcoming smells drifted from the kitchen. The dining room stove was cold to the touch and the room felt damp and closed up. Usually the men hung out at the tables for a while after supper and played cards, and the old boys appreciated a bit of heat, especially as the end of summer drew near.

I moved through the swinging doors into Drake's space and felt his presence as close as if we stood together canning corn like we had the last time I'd been here. I touched the clean counter and moved to the washstand. *Dirty dishes? Never!* Drake would never taint his reputation by leaving Jones Star Ranch with soiled pans that needed scrubbing. Glancing around I picked up on other details that I knew would drive the perfectionist around the bend. I was more convinced than ever that his departure was unplanned and spontaneous.

I heard a noise behind me and turned to discover a cowboy lurking by the entrance and staring at me. He removed his hat when I turned his way.

"Evening, Ma'am. Cook ain't in here."

"I heard. Do you know where he went?" I asked.

"No. He don't confide in me. I just hired on for the season round up."

"Oh," disappointment rang clear in my voice and the lad picked up on it.

"Did hear him mutterin' all through lunch. He thinks we're all deaf and most don't pay him any heed, but like I said, I'm new."

"What was he muttering about?" I asked.

"Mostly women. Seemed right put out about women."

My initial fears at the onset of the news came storming back. It was difficult coming to grips with him just leaving the ranch because I hadn't jumped to dump the doctor and run blindly into his vague notion of *seeing if we had a chance of being something besides friends.*

I felt the anger return, and once again my original plan when coming to Montana to steer clear of confusing men sounded like the best solution. If my conscience would not allow me to marry the doctor I certainly didn't need to take a risk like Drake. I was happy and content with my life the way it was before either of them invited their way past my defenses. Somehow I needed to get back to that place of contentment.

"Thank you. You didn't go to town with the men? Are you hungry?"

"Might be."

"Well, sit down and I'll see if I can put a cold plate together for you. The stove is not lit," I said as if the meal needed explaining. "But I'll be back in the morning to cook up a good breakfast before you head off to work."

"Big job for a little woman," he said as he straddled a chair.

"I can manage." I walked into the cold room and saw bowls and plates of prepared salads and meats on the shelves. It looked as if Drake planned to see the season out with a cold meal tomorrow. I slid the covers aside and placed a spoonful of a good variety of salads and meat on the young man's plate. After covering the dishes again, I headed back to the kitchen.

"Here you are, " I said as I passed the food to the cowboy. "Go in the dining room and relax. I won't lock up until after you leave."

I found some bacon and eggs and set them together ready for the morning. There was a large bowl of cooked potatoes and I cut them into slices. I'd add some onions and fry them up as well. That should be enough for the morning meal. Five loaves of fresh bread sat covered on a shelf. Toast and jelly should satisfy their sweet tooth. I knew that there were lots of jams available. I'd put them on the shelf myself after a scorching hot day slaving over the cook stove with Drake.

A tear escaped my eye as I recalled the special moments I'd experienced with Drake that made work seem like play. Why would he leave now? It was obvious he hadn't trusted my ability to break it off with Robert and give us a chance at love. Perhaps I should have been more upfront and told him that I cared, probably too deeply for my own good. But that very fact had been the reason for holding back. Robert was my friend and I determined to dismiss him with the respect he deserved, secretly dreading that he might discover he held second choice in my heart.

I checked the woodpile and found an ample supply piled in the shed then filled the reservoir in the stove with water. Four large coffee pots stood on the counter and I prepared the portions to perk in the morning. Looking around I debated on doing the dishes, but with no hot water available, I decided against it and just set them to soak overnight.

I'd been able to avoid the temptation to snoop behind the door at the back of the room, but now I stood and stared at it. In the end, I reasoned that it might contain a hint as to Drake's whereabouts and needed investigating. I opened the door and crept inside. The layout was simple and provided for a person's needs but little of their wants. A cot lined one wall with a small dresser beside it that served as a night table. I walked there first and sat on the edge of his neatly made bed, running my fingers along the thread of the quilted overthrow. The room had only one small window, so I lit the lantern and turned up the wick. Light spread through the room and I smiled. Everything had a place and was neatly stacked there. I pulled open the top drawer and discovered nightclothes.

The bottom drawer was another story. There were two items inside. I lifted a picture frame and turned it over. It was old and the glass was smashed in a few places. A smiling couple stared back at me through the cracks and I gasped when the truth sunk in. Drake stood beside a woman in a decorative native dress. Drake had not only been married, but he'd been married to an Indian.

Why hadn't he told me that detail? *And why should it matter*? I argued with myself. I raked my mind to remember the few specifics that he'd mentioned. Someone had burned his house with her and his son inside. Trash, he'd called them. He didn't say white trash or Indian trash – simply the word *trash* described the ones that had killed his family.

His wife was beautiful, with flawless dark skin and round almost black eyes. She peered at me as one gazing into my soul. Would she approve of Drake's affections toward me? That was silly – the woman was dead – but perhaps not to Drake. Otherwise why would he keep this photo of them in his bedside table in a drawer void of anything else? I looked closer - except this. I reached inside and picked up a loose sheet of paper that revealed a pencil drawing of a young boy holding a ball and casually leaning against a homemade batting stick. Drake had been proud to tell me of his son's skill in throwing a ball.

This was his boy. I wondered who had drawn the picture for him. If Drake had any artistic abilities, he'd never shared that knowledge with me. I toyed with the idea of taking the picture frame of the couple and have a new glass put in it and perhaps mount the drawing as well.

Then another thought hit me. If he'd planned on leaving, surely he'd have taken these personal items and his nightclothes. I leaped to my feet and hastened to the bigger chest of drawers on the other side of the room. Inside stacked in neat piles were all his shirts and pants, socks and underclothes. My heart raced. I wondered if PJ had found any signs of him on the trails close by. I closed the drawers, replaced the picture in its proper place and blew out the lantern.

I hurried from the room to find that the young cattleman had eaten and left. I placed his dishes in the water to soak and hurried from the mess hall. There was no way to lock it from the outside. I supposed Drake was always there at night and could bolt it from within. I'd have to get PJ to provide an outside lock. Someone could come in here anytime and steal all the food in one sweep.

The thought that perhaps I should move a few things down here while I did the cooking entered my mind but I knew PJ would not go for it. Yet, I was his mother and could surely make my boy see reason. What would it feel like to sleep under Drake's covers? With him gone, of course. But even breathing his space all night long presented a dangerous image in my mind and I decided I'd have to think this notion through a bit more.

Back at the homestead I paced and stared out the window until I thought I'd go crazy. I grabbed up my knitting project and perched on the edge of the settee close to a lantern. The end product would be a pink blanket for the baby girl PJ felt confident was arriving for Christmas. I smiled, for I had a similar blue blanket hidden in my room, just in case the Lord decided otherwise and gave Ruth Ellen her gender choice. From my spot I could see the drive leading to the house. I watched it more than the needles in my hands and had to unravel the yarn countless times. Finally I heard voices and ran to the window. It was dark now but I could make out the outlines of Patrick and Ruth Ellen. I picked up the lantern and ran to the door and opened it wide.

"You're back! Did you find any sign of Drake while riding?" I asked.

"Let us get inside and we'll talk, Ma. Is there any coffee left on the stove?" Patrick asked.

I ran to the kitchen and stirred up the embers. The fire blazed and I felt the pot. "Still lukewarm. Do you prefer to wait till it heats more?" I asked.

"Lukewarm is good for me," said Patrick.

"I will skip it and have a glass of cool water. Doc says I should lay off the coffee until after the baby comes. It makes me a bundle of nerves."

"Is that what does it?" Patrick said with a chuckle. "Ma, best throw the pot out in the shed for a few months. I can do without if it will keep my wife sane and less jittery."

Ruth Ellen swatted at her husband. "You're talking nonsense. I said I shouldn't drink the black poison but you can have all you want. I prefer to keep you on edge. Makes my day a sight more interesting."

Patrick looked my way, and I mouthed the word, *patience*. He sighed and plunked down onto a kitchen chair.

"Anyway, about Drake. No signs of the man, but we did find other odd clues that are new to the area."

"Such as?" I asked.

"Indian arrows. Haven't seen them hereabouts in years. There's only one tribe that live in the area and they tend to keep to themselves. Holed up all summer in some hunting and fishing paradise that most fellas would love to invade, but keep clear of."

"Wise decision," I said. "Is the tribe hostile?" I'd never considered the threat of Indians when I agreed to come West.

"Naw, most folks have learned that it's better to give the whites and natives their own spaces and not interfere. Too much bloodshed in the past between the two and the Chief is a wise man, or so I'm told. Only know him by reputation."

"Maybe Drake knows him," Ruth Ellen said. "That might be where he's headed. If an angry brave were chasing him, and shooting arrows his way perhaps we should be concerned."

"There's no reason to think Drake associates with the tribe. He's been working with me on the ranch since I first came," Patrick said.

"Do you know anything of his past? Perhaps there was a connection." I was fishing – letting Patrick do the thinking before I enlightened him on what I knew for certain.

Patrick shrugged his shoulders. "Think he said he was married once but she died. He's pretty tight lipped about his life before arriving at the Jones Star Ranch."

"You both know I went to the mess hall to prepare for tomorrows breakfast." They nodded and I continued. "Well, when I was done I thought if I went through Drake's room I might find a clue as to his sudden departure."

"Oh my, you are brave to shuffle through a man's things," said Ruth Ellen. "Did you find anything that might help?"

"I didn't think so, until now. You talking about arrows where they shouldn't be might be a bigger clue than you think. I found a picture of Drake with his wife in the bottom drawer. She was an Indian. And he told me once that someone had set fire to his cabin when he was gone and burned her and his son inside."

Patrick let the front legs of his chair drop to the floor and bent over the table. "You don't say. I never knew any of that."

"Do you suppose he's in trouble? Why would he go back there now after all these years?" I asked.

"Something new must have happened for him to leave so suddenly. PJ, whatever shall we do?" Ruth Ellen asked.

"I will go in and talk to the Sheriff tomorrow. See if he's heard of any uprisings. Or maybe he knew Drake way back then and can remember the circumstances around his wife's death."

Suddenly I wanted more than anything to stay at the mess hall. I wanted to be there should Drake find his way back home safe and sound.

"PJ, I'm considering moving a few things into the back room at the kitchen. It will be easier to live there while I cook for the men. I can imagine I will spend a lot of time preparing meals. It will take some getting used to feeding such a number three times a day."

"Definitely not!"

"The men are Cowboys, Ma. Not always polite and polished. You don't need to be around that."

"I am not glass and I will not break, PJ, because of an earful of foul talk and rude behavior."

"I was willing to let you do days, but not nights, Ma. I won't budge. We will come to the mess hall for supper each night and Ruth Ellen will help you clean up and walk back to the house with you."

"There is no lock on the outside of the building. Anyone can walk in and help themselves to all the food," I said.

"I can remedy that. Jimmy will install a lock tomorrow and we will shut the dining hall up tight before we head up to the house at night. The boys can sit and play cards in the bunk house till we find a replacement for Drake."

"A replacement?" I clutched a fist to my heart. "Please PJ, we need to find him first and if he chooses to stay away, at least we can return his personal items to him. He left without his clothes. That has to indicate he's in trouble."

"Ma, sounds to me like you made your choice in men, but,

have you told the Doc yet?" Patrick asked.

"He's supposed to come calling this week but he hasn't shown his face as of yet. Sunday was hardly an appropriate time with the boy's injuries and then Agnes falling ill. I do intend to break it off with him."

"Why is this the first I've heard of such nonsense? Ma, you and the doctor are simply perfect for one another," said Ruth Ellen.

Patrick wrapped an arm around his wife. "Now, Ruthie, don't go interfering. Ma has a mind of her own and she can plan her own life."

"Does that mean you'll stay on with us? Now I can live with that news..." Her hand flew to her mouth as it all sank in. "Drake! Ma you have feelings for the cook?"

"Something closer akin to love than I feel for Robert, but we were still getting to know one another. He left before I had the chance to settle the affair with Robert. When you first told me the news of Drake's running off I feared that he was escaping the idea of us, but now I don't know. My heart and head are in a muddle."

"That's love, Ma. Best resign to it now and let it flow." Ruth Ellen placed her head in the hollow of her husband's neck. "I caused such grief between PJ and me simply because I refused to face the inevitable. Love always wins, and one partner will lead the other home. Maybe you're the leader for this stretch of the process."

"That's an interesting way of unraveling the mystery of love," I said.

"All I can say, Ma, is that the journey there is sometimes painful, but worth it in the end," said Patrick.

"In all cases?" I asked, dubious that I'd ever find love in Drake's arms.

"Suppose not. But everlasting love is found in the face of

God. Anything earthly is a temporary blessing." Patrick said.

"You are a wise man," I said, proud to hear such wisdom from his young lips.

"Lessons learned from the Good Book and life, that's all." Patrick shifted in his seat. "Are you ready to hit the hay, wife. I'm dog tired."

"Speaking of dogs, have either of you seen Scrapper lately? She never came up for table leavings this morning and she didn't come around the barn all day."

"I know she likes to hang out at the mess hall," I said. "Drake offers more treats than we do so she's probably switched her allegiance to him."

"Not likely! Scrapper is my dog and she'd never abandon me for a man – even one that spoils her with food."

"There is a bond between you two, for sure," said Patrick. "Let's all keep an eye out tomorrow. She's probably out chasing varmints and birds off the newly mowed field. Tying the hay tomorrow for winter cattle feed."

"You pair head off to bed. I'll close up and get the morning coffee ready. I'll be headed to the mess hall before sunup to get started on bacon, eggs and fried potatoes."

"Skip the coffee up here Ma, and we'll come to you for breakfast."

"I'll show up in time to make the toast and set the table, Ma. I'm not so good at sunup these days."

The house was quiet when I wandered up the steps to my room. What was keeping the doctor away all week? I wanted more than ever to wipe the slate clean for us. I had an idea that Stacy Trop would waste no time replacing me at the altar. And I was at peace with that thought. *They* would be the *perfect couple*, to use Ruth Ellen's words, even if Robert had not yet come to realize it. A similar work interest, a more than obvious attraction on Stacy's part, and the fact that she made his face come alive just being in the same room with him, were prime ingredients to something deeper lurking within. Agnes had hit the nail on the head – in a relationship, simply living with someone would never suffice; one needed to find that perfect someone they could not live without.

    I'd learned that valuable difference over this past month and now with Drake's disappearance, I wondered if it were too late for us.

Chapter 9

My days took on a busy routine of early mornings, long days and falling exhausted into bed at the absurd hour that mothers would be tucking their children under the covers for the night. No nightlife for me. Then again, that did not seem to be a problem. Robert stayed clear of the ranch, and inside, the chicken-in-me relished that fact. Confronting him about our love life – or lack thereof – drained me just to think about it. So the days pressed on, and I functioned and served the men at the mess hall with a proficiency that came easily to me. The kitchen was my comfort zone. The hired men responded well and despite Patrick's concerns, treated me with the utmost respect and appreciation.

It was md-afternoon when the news came about Drake. Patrick delivered it. We sat together at the small table inside the mess hall kitchen with our coffee.

"Ma, Sherriff returned to town this morning. He found the dog and Drake."

I hated the expression of dread on his face and gulped the hot liquid to satisfy a need for comfort more than thirst.

"They followed the trail to the Indian camp. Stayed hid on their bellies on top of a hill and watched them as they went about their business. Wasn't long before Drake came out of a tent and joined them. Interacted with a few but the Sheriff didn't witness any hostility. He concluded Drake was there of his own free will. So, he left him and headed back to Aspen Glen."

"At least, he's not dead and we know where he is." My voice recognized relief in that knowledge but my heart ached at the loss of a possibility of us. "You mentioned the dog; did you mean Scrapper?"

"Unfortunately. The Deputy darted off the trail to relieve himself and found Scrapper tossed in the bushes with an arrow through him. Must have followed Drake and got caught up in a skirmish with an Indian. Someone took the time to cover him with a blanket. I'm guessing that was Drake."

"How is Ruth Ellen taking the news?"

"Not well. Lots of tears, but she is trying to understand that dogs roaming free are prey to anything in the West. The next one she assures me will be a house dog." He shook his head. "Not too keen about that idea. Anyway, you are invited to a burial this evening. Maybe that will help her put Scrapper to rest."

"Possibly, but time will be the cure. And a new puppy, should you come around to her way of thinking." I smiled and Patrick grimaced.

"But, back to Drake. It bothers me that we still don't know why he's decided to leave and live in an Indian camp," Patrick said. "Why couldn't he tell us beforehand so we wouldn't wonder? I like the man and hate to leave his departure a mystery."

"Maybe it has something to do with the arrows you found? It might not have been his choice, initially," I said, silently grieving that he'd chosen them over us. "Would it not have been appropriate for the Sherriff to go into the camp and have a meeting with Drake?"

"Probably didn't want to stir up trouble. The agreement with the Indian is that we leave one another alone. Sheriff saw the bloodshed years back and wouldn't risk a repeat of it just to satisfy our curiosity."

"I suppose Drake is a big boy and can look after himself," I said, sadness tainting every word.

"What about you, Ma? How is your heart doing?"

I chuckled. "What does that matter? I am still promised to another man – one that has obviously forgotten I exist. PJ, have you heard of any emergencies the doctor is tending to away from Aspen Glen?"

"Granny says he goes in and out of his office every day. His usual busy, but he still comes home every night."

"I think I need to go to town," I said and then remembered my new responsibility. "But I'm so busy here."

"My wife has hired Jillian to come clean the homestead once a week to take that burden off the shoulders of you ladies. I'm sure Ruth Ellen will come and fill in for an afternoon if you need to go to town."

"But what if I miss him. It would be a wasted trip, and I do not want to tire your wife for no reason."

Patrick laughed. "She is getting rather huge out front, isn't she? Do you think God put a girl and a boy in there to satisfy us both?"

"I've never heard of twins in our family or the Thorncrest's, so it's not likely. Perhaps the baby is going to come out half grown instead," I suggested playfully.

"Ruthie has such a small frame. Not like some of the robust women hereabouts," Patrick said, worry lines etching his face. "Heard terrible things about big babies and little ladies."

I patted his hand. "Not to worry, Son. She has an excellent

doctor, and now a mid-wife to tend to the birthing."

"Did you want to go to town today? It'll keep Ruth Ellen busy here and not moping around mourning after her dog," Patrick asked – then quickly added. "You realize you could still have the marriage, now that Drake appears to be staying gone."

"That wouldn't be fair, PJ, and you know it. He deserves the kind of love that you and Ruthie have, not a second-rate replacement."

"And you – what will you do?"

"I'm going to apply for this job. Do you think the boss of Jones Star Ranch will hire me?"

"Ma, you don't need to work."

"Maybe not, but a single woman likes a little bit of independence. And I'd still be nice and close to my grandbabies but not underfoot and meddlesome. I've been thinking about it and it's what I want to do, PJ."

"You've certainly won the men over - everything good to say about the food, the new cook and even your posted table rules. I'd never have believed they'd cater to your guidelines if I hadn't heard praise come from the worst hellion of the bunch."

"Good. Then it's settled." I giggled impulsively. I'd never had an outside-the-home job in my entire life. "How much do you pay?"

Patrick laughed. "Straight to the point. I like that in a hired hand. Pay is room and board, and for you, fifty dollars a month."

"That's a lot! I don't want special treatment. But, more to the point, can you afford me?" I asked.

"If I can't, your daughter-in-law can. She is itching to use some of that money she's inherited. The Jones Star ranch is doing well, Ma. And as long as you keep feeding my men and they continue to work hard, you will be well worth it. What will you do with your money anyway?"

"First off, I'd like an advance. Since the weather will be changing soon, I want to hire someone to come and expand the back room. I'd like a proper sitting area, a sewing room because that can get to be quite a mess, and one of those inside toilets put in the woodshed."

"I can do that for you, Ma. You don't need to spend your hard earned money on a renovation."

"Not your obligation. If the room was good enough for Drake in the past, it's good enough for your new hire."

Patrick laughed. "Except that she wants to expand the space to accommodate all her stuff?"

"With my money – don't forget that," I said. "You'll not pay a penny to pamper me here. I won't have the boys grumbling favoritism and causing you unnecessary ribbing or grief on your own ranch."

"They wouldn't dare. I am the boss and you are my mother. They will come to grips with that or hit the road out of here." Patrick was unyielding, not a side I'd seen of him often. I supposed that's why he was a successful businessman. He knew when to be charitable and when to stand solid.

I jumped to my feet, suddenly excited about my future. It was a good compromise. If I couldn't have Drake, I'd not have anyone, and that was that. I sincerely hoped this newest decision would stick better than the ones I'd affirmed lately.

"Let me know if Ruth Ellen is available. I have most of the supper meal set out and ready to go on the stove. She won't have too much preparation at all. And tell her to leave the dishes soaking and I'll clean up in the morning." As an afterthought I blurted out. "Oh, the burial! Perhaps we can have the ceremony when we do our nightly talk with the Creator tonight. I'll be sure to be home before dark. How long could it possibly take to break a man's heart?" My voice attempted to make light of my mission but my heart ached and prayed for an agreeable parting.

"You appear to have been revived, Ma. If I'd known you wanted to get paid for your services I'd have provided it long ago."

"Oh, not paid for labor in my son's home. Never! But a career woman – now that's something to get excited about. I've never had much money of my own to spend on whatever I want. The bit of sewing and cleaning I did for homes in Boston always had to go toward paying rent and putting food on my table. I get that here free, as part of my wages! I am so excited, PJ. The only damper is that my blessing will be mine alone, but in time, I will learn to love that too."

"Drake is already in your past, then?"

"No, Son. The man has stolen my heart and whether he is here or not, I will always love him. I feel he was my soul mate, but he left before we had a chance to discover it."

"One day at a time, right, Ma? That's what you always say."

"Yes, one day at a time. And this one is indeed a bittersweet mix of both loss and gain." I sighed deep for the day was not over yet. "I hope Robert accepts my change of mind and is able to move on. I never wanted to hurt the man."

"He's a big boy. The doctor will see your bleeding heart of hearts and forgive you. Then you can both revert back to the friends that you were meant to be."

"I do hope so," I said.

"Go and get all gussied up – bad news always sounds better coming from a beautiful woman – and I will run and fetch Ruth Ellen from yonder barn and bring her over here. Then I'll hitch the team and bring the carriage around to the house for you."

"We women keep you hopping, don't we?"

"Wouldn't have it any other way. Now off with you before I change my mind about this whole career idea," Patrick said as he dropped his cup in the wash pan and hurried out the door. I followed close on his heels, anxious to end this day with grace and start my new adventure fresh and guilt free.

In town I parked in front of the Mercantile and headed inside. When Agnes caught sight of me she hurried from the back of the store where she was packing shelves. Her hug was strong and sincere.

"Clare, nice to see you. How are things out at the ranch?"

"Do you have time for tea at the Diner? I could use a listening ear," I asked.

"Certainly. I always make time for family. Let me tell Stanley where I'm going. Be right back." She disappeared behind a curtain just as the door chimes sounded. Of all people, Stacy Trop marched in.

"Mrs. Jones, so glad to catch up with you. I think we need to chat."

I looked at the determination on her face and decided against it. "As a matter of fact, I am in town to see Robert. But now I'm off to the Diner with Agnes. That's all I have time to squeeze in today. I'm afraid, our chat will have to wait." I held her gaze.

"Robert is busy today." She stood steady and unrelenting while continuing to glare at me.

"He will see me. Tell him I will be at the office within the hour." I never backed down and the woman appeared surprised that she could not overpower me. "Don't look at me like that, for I don't want to think ill of you when we've hardly had a chance to get acquainted. I realize the doctor holds high regard for you, as he should, and I respect that. We need not become enemies, so please, don't pick a fight where none is required."

The woman relaxed her rigid stance and plastered on a fake grin. It didn't brighten her face as her smiles usually did, so I assumed the effort was forced for my benefit. I had no intention of being manipulated or ordered about by this woman who apparently saw herself as the doctor's new guardian. He certainly did not need her protection, but in time, if it were meant to be, she'd learn of the man's real needs. I did not relent in my mission. Any thing she may wish to discuss with me was none of her business. Robert was my first and only responsibility. I'd let him deal with Stacy Trop as he saw fit.

A voice from behind sounded. "Stanley, you have a customer." Agnes came and scooped her arm through mine and said. "Shall we be off? We've so much catching up to do." I witnessed Agnes cast a stern gaze at the woman who stood by watching our departure. The owner of the store pushed her head a bit higher as she passed by.

I laughed as soon as we turned and headed down the boardwalk. "Agnes, if I didn't know you better, I'd call you a snob."

"Fiddle-e-Dee. The woman is too high on herself if you ask me. She needs to be knocked down a peg or two if she's to fit into this community."

"I tried," I confessed.

"And I heard! Cheered you on the whole time." Agnes laughed. "But on a more pleasant note, as you've probably heard, Mary, my cook has been baking up a storm for Abigail's customers. Gets paid a tidy sum from the Diner for the goods she delivers daily. You must try her raspberry scones. They are to die for."

"A figure of speech, right – to die for?" I asked in fun.

"Definitely. The woman would lose all her customers if we keeled over dead while sinking our teeth into the scrumptious bait."

"You seem rather joyful this afternoon," I said.

"Easy when you're so happy you could burst out of these

corsets. I've been debating on letting this old-lady-flab flow free. What do you think?"

I chuckled. "That would be a personal preference. Whatever suits you and Stanley will have to suit the rest of the world."

"Right on! Now you're getting it straight." She sobered slightly. "From this unexpected visit, I gather that you've made a decision about your love life and have summoned the old and wise for her opinion?" she asked.

"Mrs. Fischer, you are absolutely correct in your assumption."

"Good! I always say, make the decision, act on it and move forward. It's the only way to stay ahead of the game." Agnes held the door of Abigail's Diner and ushered me in. Once seated, the server approached our table. Agnes ordered for us. "We want two cups of hot tea with a touch of milk and two of Mary's biggest and fruitiest, raspberry scones."

"Coming right up, ladies."

Within a few minutes I was chowing down on the best tasting treat I'd ever tasted. "Mm, this is so good. I will have to see if I can steal a few recipes from your cook for my new enterprise."

"Your new enterprise?"

"PJ has hired me to cook for his men down at the mess hall. I am so excited. I have never in all my life, secured a real job, and I'm discovering that it makes one feel rather fulfilled. Imagine someone actually paying me for doing what I love."

"I am thrilled for you, I think." Agnes screwed up her eyebrows. "Doesn't Patrick employ Drake for that task– the other man in your life?"

"That's the bad news I'm afraid. Drake disappeared without a word, leaving all his belongings behind. I feared the worst at the beginning, but the Sheriff followed his trail and it appears he has settled in with a band of Indians. The law saw no reason to attempt to rescue a man who walked freely amongst them. I understand the peace treaty between the white man and Indian is fragile, and both walk on egg shells to avoid a repeat bloodbath of yesteryear."

"Drake has chosen to leave the ranch and live with Indians? I can't believe that." She took another bite of her scone and washed it down with a sip of tea.

"I had a hard time as well. I was secretly hoping that something might develop with Drake and me – of course, after I inform the good doctor that he is a free man again. But now I've resolved to live alone, at the mess hall, and still close to my family, earn a living and do good works in the community. That sounds fulfilling, right?"

"Perhaps for the right woman."

"Oh, please don't reopen the scars. I need to put Drake behind me if I'm to move on. He obviously does not want the same things in life that I do, so we are better off apart."

"A perfect solution for today. But don't cling to martyrdom, dear. You are too young to settle for a loveless life. There is no reason why you can't have it all just like me. Career, home, husband, family… the works."

"I shall watch my door for the next eligible bachelor that sets my heart racing and sends earth-shattering tingles down my spine." I laughed as I reminded her of her of our earlier discussion.

"Ah yes… I for one live for the tingles." Agnes laughed. "And I will pray they find you as well."

One hour later I walked into the doctor's office. He was busy with a patient and Stacy was nowhere to be seen. Good. I didn't want to have to drag Robert away in order to talk, but knew I'd do it in a heartbeat to avoid his nurse's ears glued to the closed door.

Robert looked almost embarrassed when he glanced up and saw me enter. "Be with you in a minute, Clare. Just bandaging up a scrape for this youngster."

"I'll wait." I went to the stove and poured two cups of coffee. Bad news always washed down easier with the comforting drink – or at least I hoped so. I brought them to the table and sat down.

"Thanks, Doc," the child yelled as the door slammed behind him.

And then we were alone. We both started to talk at the same time. I allowed him to speak first.

"Sorry, I've not been out to the ranch. Busy here all the time, it seems." His fingers fidgeted with the mug handle and then after spouting his excuse, he buried his mouth in the cup opening and slurped loudly.

"I understand completely. That's why I made the trip here. But, we do need to talk, Robert," I said.

"It's your turn. Go ahead." He seemed relieved and I drew courage from his discomfort. Surely he'd see we were not meant for anything other than friendship.

"Robert, you know I admire you greatly and have strong feelings for you." When his eyes bolted to my face I added, "as a friend." Now it was his turn to squirm. "I wonder if we have forced our relationship beyond a place of comfort – for both of us. Our times together while courting have been awkward to say the least and to be honest, I miss my friend."

Emotion stuck somewhere in my throat and I paused involuntarily. I felt his hands cover mine and looked up to find the man wearing a warm smile – the one I treasured and had not seen for weeks.

"My dear brave Clare. I am embarrassed that you had to come and tell me this when we both knew our hearts were faltering over our decision to wed. I am the man and should have taken this lead. I'm sorry."

"It only matters that we bare our hearts openly now and move into the destiny designed for us with or without the confines of marriage."

"Well said, Clare. Now I know why you were the one to take the lead. I would have fumbled the words for sure."

We both laughed and the burden of nearly making the biggest mistake of our lives fell from our shoulders.

"Perhaps someday we shall both find love. But in the meantime, you and I, Robert Palatsie, will always remain the best of friends. And on your special day – with the woman who steals your heart – I will stand with you and applaud because that's what friends do."

I felt no need to bring up Stacy or Drake. They were on the sidelines of our lives, and their stories were in the making. They were not the cause of this breakup, and we both could rest our conscience that this was the best decision for the doctor and Mrs. Jones.

I raised my cup and he clinked his with mine. "Cheers, dear friend. May our lives unfold as the Good Lord leads."

"Amen," agreed Robert. He rose immediately and I followed suit. He rushed over to my side of the table and pulled me into his arms. Everything felt right in his embrace and I was pleased and relieved to acknowledge the lack of tingles going up and down my spine. But I did feel love of a different kind envelop me – the kind that good friends share.

I pushed myself out to arm's length and whispered, "Perfect!" just as the door swung shut with a slam. Stacy stood at the entrance, speechless and frozen to the spot.

"Good day to you, Doctor." I called out as I headed toward the door. When I passed alongside the stunned woman, I leaned close. "Good luck, Stacy Trop. The doctor is a mighty good catch for the right woman."

Chapter 10

When I left the doctor's office I ran headlong into Gerald, dressed in his work clothes. "Well, hello. Where are you off to in such a hurry?

"I am off to the Mercantile. Running low on supplies for the shop and need to stock up."

"How is your young apprentice working out?"

"He is a God-send. Frees me up to pursue other matters of interest." He winked and I suspected he implied his quest to win the schoolteacher's attention.

"Good luck with that. I want you to be the first to know that the good doctor and I have decided that walking down the aisle was never meant to be and have parted as friends for life – just as it should be."

"Ya sound mighty happy fer a gal being jilted."

I laughed. "Truth is, we both agreed this is for the best. So the only blame falls to the fact that we ever began this whole façade." I was so excited I couldn't stop the flow. "And I am extra delighted to run into you. Can you direct me to a carpenter? I need to have some work done on my new place of business."

"Well, I'd love to share the one I hired but he'll find it hard pressed to get my new place closed in before the snow flies. But, if it's not too big a job, Jake, Stanley's brother that works part time at the Mercantile, might want to take it on. He's good with wood."

"What a splendid idea! I never even thought of him. His hours must be cut big time now that the newlyweds are home and minding the store."

"And the new business you was referrin' to is..." Gerald prompted me.

"You are looking at the new cook at the Jones Star Ranch mess hall." I decided to finish the story before he asked. "Drake, it appears, has had a change of heart and has decided to return to live amongst the Indians."

"Indians?"

"It's a long story. You'll have to come for dinner. We're all eating at the mess hall these days and you are most welcome to join us. We usually eat after the men, around 6:30. Come any night – just show up. I cook plenty." I looped my arm through his. "Now, let's get to the Mercantile and see to the needs of our businesses."

That night three of us gathered next to a small mound of dirt behind the homestead in a fenced in plot of land that had been designated for family burials. Patrick had nailed a box together and laid Scrapper's remains inside. The lid was nailed shut. I understood the reason why because of the smell that drifted upward. Decay had already begun to deteriorate his body. Poor Ruth Ellen did not even get to hug her pet one last time. Patrick lowered the box in the hole and looked at his wife.

"Would you like to say a few words, Ruthie?" he asked.

She bit her lower lip to stop it from trembling, and nodded, yes. The words came slow and painful at first but soon took on a peace I recognized as comfort from the Lord.

"Scrapper was a gift, not only from my husband but from God who knew that I would soon cling to the animal for support during my recovery from the accident that caused memory loss. Scrapper never gave up on me and I grew to love her a second time, just as I did PJ – both endowments from the Creator of the stars, sent to help heal at the most vulnerable time in my life." Her voice choked and Patrick took up the tribute.

"Thankful for the laughs she created at home with her silly antics and for the critters she brought down that threatened the ranch," Patrick said.

I decided to add my bit when I saw Ruth Ellen's smile. "And for those adorable eyes that begged at the back door for table scraps and her grateful wagging tail that taught us all to show appreciation for the little things in life."

"Yes Lord, and for this short time with Scrapper, we thank you. And now we ask that she know peace in this resting place provided for her," Ruth Ellen said.

"In Jesus name, Amen," ended Patrick.

We all took turns to throw one shovel of the dirt into the hole on top of the box. I gathered Ruth Ellen in my arms and walked with her toward the porch. Patrick would complete the burial.

The next morning after serving breakfast to the men, Jake and I began planning the addition. We paced off the new part and discussed the project. The new section would include a smaller sewing room on one end and my bedroom running the full length of the structure and sidling up against the wood shed. It would be easy to put a door into the new privy from both my room and the kitchen-woodshed side. The outside door would have a strong lock to keep me safe inside my new home. It felt funny to think of Drake's space as my new home – in fact I'd never given a home, apart from PJ's, a second thought since coming to Montana.

The one room that presently existed would serve as a sitting room and Jake was cutting a bigger window to allow more daylight into the room and I'd ordered a potbelly stove to help heat the area come wintertime. I did not relish the idea of leaving the door to my living quarters open to the main kitchen just for the purpose of warmth from the cook-stove. A woman's privacy did not seem too much to ask for.

Jake left again for town with a long list of items to order from the mill and the Fischer's Mercantile, and a promise to start the groundwork as soon as possible. Agnes and Francine both offered a few pieces of elaborate furnishings and touches from Boston and I conceded to the fuss they made over me. Part of me wanted to keep it rustic, so in the end I decided to mix the décor to include both worlds. I did not want to wipe away Drake's presence in this place totally.

Moving forward should have felt perfect. Instead it drug up where Drake was concerned. I'd not settled in my mind that he would choose to live with the Indians, not after working at the ranch. I even dared to hope that I possessed a touch of drawing power – but alas, if I did, it appeared not to be enough. A random thought crossed my mind and I gasped aloud when the impression took form in my intellect. Perhaps his wife never burned in the fire and was kept from him all these years for some unknown reason. Indians may not have liked the idea of a squaw marrying a white man. It sounded reasonable. Why else would Drake not return home to Aspen Glen but that he'd been reunited with his lost love? Feasible, I supposed, but not necessarily gratifying for my heart. Yet his happiness was my first and only concern and I know he had loved his first wife. So be it.

I wandered throughout the kitchen aimlessly, the lull before the storm of lunch activity. Picking up a spatula, I recalled the day that Drake had playfully swatted my hand with it as I'd worked alongside him in this room. Never a moment went by while working in his space that some reminder of him sprang up to taunt me, either causing a smile or to tear-up with regret. Would I ever make the transfer in my mind and acknowledge his kitchen as mine? No. The mind, although it held many memories, was not the problem. It was an issue of the heart. Unaware to me, I'd fallen in love with Drake under this very roof. I hoped that in time the realization would bring me comfort.

I decided to move in before the renovation was complete. The main room was still intact and I secretly yearned to crawl under Drake's blankets just once before the cot disappeared into the sewing room and the lush furnishings would take its place. It took a lot of persuasion, but finally Patrick agreed. But, not before escorting me to all the surrounding buildings and making sure I knew all the nearby paths by heart, especially the one that led to the men's bunkhouse. It stood closer than the homestead should I need emergency help of any kind. We ate our evening meal together and Ruth Ellen helped me with the clean up.

"Are you not just a teeny bit fearful, Ma, to be in here alone at night?" Ruth Ellen asked.

"Not in the least. God will not allow anything not ordained of him to happen to me. I believe that and it gives me the peace I need to carry on through the changes of life."

"And you've had so many," She impulsively kissed my cheek. "You are a wonderful woman and I am blessed to call you family."

"Why thank you, dear. You likewise." My heart swelled with pride. "My son made a perfect choice when he snatched up the new Mrs. Jones."

"I am crazy-happy. The recent trip back to Boston only made me realize how much I love it here in Montana. I would have dried up like an old prune with any husband other than PJ, especially one in the city."

Patrick instructed Jake to make a double latch that I could lock from the inside of the kitchen and outside should I choose to go out for the evening. Time only permitted the main door's locks to be installed today, and much to my son's dismay, we had to wait for the lock to go on the back woodshed entrance tomorrow."

Patrick entered the room apparently pleased with himself." I know exactly how to fix the problem, for tonight anyway." With a long piece of wood and hammer in hand, he marched through the pantry door into the woodshed. The board covered both the door and the jam. He nailed me in.

I watched with a smile on my face. "Perhaps you should leave the tool there in case this is my only door of escape should a fire occur."

"Heaven forbid, Ma," Ruth Ellen gasped. "Patrick, is the stove chimney clean of soot and such flammable things?"

"The men clean it on a regular basis; nothing to worry about there. It's a new stove last year."

"Good. See Ma, nothing to worry about there. PJ looks after us so well," she said as she cozied up next to him and planted a kiss on his lips. "I'm tired, husband. Are you ready for bed?"

"I am, just as soon as we all step outside and talk to the Creator of the Stars. It will be harder to manage this tradition as a family when we don't live in the same house," Patrick said.

"We all live under the stars, Son. Whether we hold hands as one or not, we will all petition the Lord together every night. You can be sure of that." I witnessed the relief in his face and knew how important this Jones ritual had become to him.

Ruth Ellen grabbed both our hands and pulled us outside the kitchen door, the only one not nailed shut. "Let's get to it, Mr. Jones. The evening is chilly and I don't want your baby to catch a cold."

We all laughed as she rubbed her swollen belly and moaned theatrically.

When finished, Patrick remained outside the door until he heard the latch pull across into lock position. He rattled the door and when satisfied he could not get inside yelled "Goodnight, Ma," and he and his wife headed to the homestead.

I turned and looked at the neat kitchen. Drake would be pleased. I chided myself. When would these thoughts cease to enter my mind? All that mattered anymore was that I was pleased. I lifted the lantern from the counter, turned up the wick, and proceeded into the small adjoining room. This would be the last night it would hold the now familiar touches of Drake. Tomorrow Jake would cut the doors into the new space and the rooms would be redefined. It was for the best. Moving forward I needed to see this as my space alone.

Bags and boxes containing my personal belongings and the few cherished items I'd brought from Boston sat piled on the floor. No sense unpacking it now. The time to sort through it all would come after the furnishings for the bedroom arrived from my supportive friends, Agnes and Francine. The unveiling would be Thursday, and the ladies and I had a full day planned of decorating and making the new space feel like mine. Ruth Ellen had agreed to do kitchen duty and I'd been working ahead to make her load less burdensome.

After rummaging through my luggage for a clean outfit, I spread my clothes out for tomorrow. My entire wardrobe was small but simple, befitting a woman embarking on a profession involving kitchen duty. I probably owned more aprons than dresses. The white smock soiled first, so as long as they were clean and fresh, the dress underneath could be worn a couple times with no one the wiser.

I wondered if a washtub hung in the woodshed. I'd be solely responsible to launder my clothes in the future, and surely

Drake had need of one in the past. I speculated if Jillian would start doing the family's clothes up in the homestead. I snickered aloud. Ruth Ellen was the woman of the house and she'd figure it all out.

I groaned. A quick bath would feel good tonight. The kitchen was still hot during the day as the warm weather lingered into September. I checked and there was plenty of heated water in the reservoir. When I found the fragrant soap easily the decision was made. It was too early to go to sleep anyway. My mind was still in a tizzy considering my new world, and I marveled at the freedom that penetrated my senses. In Boston, living alone had never offered such happiness – but the past was behind me. I loved my life in Montana, despite failing in love, and a bath, on this important night of new beginnings, would serve to skim off any layers that threatened to weigh me down.

I held the lantern high, walked into the kitchen and out into the woodshed. The door remained nailed shut and there was no tub hanging on the wall. I wondered if it had been hung on the back porch. Such a nuisance.

When the disappointment overwhelmed me, I again went to the kitchen and opened the main door. Stepping outside I drank in the freshness of the clear night. A bright moon and endless stars illuminated the sky and I reveled in it for a brief moment. Remembering PJ's warnings, I quickened to the back porch, and exhaled deeply, relieved and rewarded when I caught sight of the sought-after bathtub hanging from a nail on the wall. I dragged it down and while balancing both the lantern and the tin tub, hurried back inside. I pushed it across the floor and relocked the main door.

I exhaled, long and hard. Silly! Unknowingly, I'd allowed PJ and Ruth Ellen's fears to infiltrate my peace, and it chose now to rear its ugly head. I refused to feel nervous living in these new surroundings, and I harbored no intentions of remaining indoors for the rest of my life.

I flung my rebuke into the air. "This is my freedom and you will not take it from me." I stomped my foot for effect and grabbed the washbasin.

Close to the stove I poured the tub quarter full with warm water and closed the curtains covering the two windows in the room. Grabbing a soft flannel nightdress from my trunk, I brought it into the kitchen and began the process of slipping out of my dress and stepping into the tub. For some reason I felt rushed and awkward bathing in this room. In the future, I'd do it in my bedroom, even if I had to drag pails of water from the kitchen, through my sitting room, clear to the far side of my living quarters. I stood and lathered my body then swept down to rinse off. The stress was rising from within and I was steadily losing the sense of delightful anticipation that I'd felt at the onset. The bath idea had somehow turned sour. I stepped out and towel dried as if time were not on my side and slipped the clean cotton gown over my head, and as my nostrils filled with the fragrance of the windblown material, that one action managed to free me of the spell I'd fallen under

I looked down at the basin. Now what? I did not want to face soapy dirty water first thing in the morning. I sighed and looked toward the door. It was a long drag but the water needed to be dumped outside. Perhaps an evening bath was not the greatest idea I'd had lately. Living alone did present some inconveniences.

With two hands I grabbed the handle and dragged it toward the door. I unlocked it and backed out with the tub passing the threshold last. Not wanting to create a puddle at the doorstep, I dragged it further down the wrap around porch then stood straight to decide my next step. With sadness I resigned that, when full of water, the tub was too heavy for me. It would have to wait for the morning for some strong gent to dump. I'd bribe some eager cowboy with an extra cinnamon roll.

    I shivered in the evening breeze and turned back toward the door. Hurrying inside, I again bolted the door, grabbed up the lantern and made a dash for the warmth of the cot. It helped to think of it that way. Not Drake's bed, but the cot. I did not want to lie awake basking in any scent that the man might have left under the covers. Or perhaps I did. Who could truly know the mind or the heart?

    I extinguished the lantern and jumped under the covers. Sure enough, an all too familiar smell wafted from the pillow and my heart ached, but only for a moment. A peace flooded over me and I snuggled deeper.

    The room was dark and only a small beam of moonlight shone in through the thin curtains. I'd have to hang new drapery, although in its defense, the new day dawning in my face would never allow me to sleep in. I wondered if I'd hear the rooster from PJ's barn. No – the outbuildings that serviced the men's needs were closer and that's where I acquired the eggs used in the mess hall. Just before I drifted off to sleep, I prayed that rooster would crow on time. The wake-up call had become my alarm clock and it would not do my reputation well to be late for breakfast preparations on this first day of living at the dining hall.

    Somewhere between asleep and awake I sensed shadows moving about. No noise accompanied the presence. The movements were soundless, hard to separate, like a gentle breeze breathing though the trees. My senses piqued but I refused to open my eyes, as if not acknowledging the presence would produce less danger than meeting it head on. Suddenly the shadows that crossed my closed eyelids stopped moving and I held my breath. The decision was taken from me when a voice invaded the eerie silence.

"Get up!" The order was cut and dry, spoken with an unfamiliar accent.

My eyes bolted open and in the faint moonlight, stood a young man – dressed in Indian garb with stripes of paint smeared across his face. I sat upright and brought a hand to my face to smother the scream. The reaction was instinctive, but perhaps the better idea would have been to let it rip. When I did not move he grabbed my hand and dragged me from the cot. His strength easily surpassed my ability to balance on my two feet. I stumbled to the floor. He continued to drag me. Backbone from within stirred and I yelled.

"Let go of me!"

I'm sure it was not fear that flickered across his features – perhaps, more one of surprise. Regardless of the source, it caused him to about face and look down his long nose at his struggling captive. The young man's eyes were dark, almost black and outlined with white paint. I recalled stories I'd read of Indians kidnapping white girls who had never been seen or heard from again. Or on the brighter side, miraculously rescued by concerned family and friends. The women, although planted back into white society, were never quite the same after being taken prisoner by the Indians. I was confident that I'd fall into the second category should this continue in his favor. I had no doubt he'd have the last word.

"You come!" He was fixated with his mission and began to drag me again. I wiggled loose and stood to my feet. The same confused expression crossed his face and then I noticed the likeness. He displayed Drake's features, masked by those of a sinister intensity. Could this be Drake's son? If the wife had not died, perhaps the son hadn't either.

He could speak English so I'd ask him. "What do you want?"

He scanned the room as if suddenly remembering that he

came for something else and found me instead. He moved through the room at lightning speed, tossing Drake's clothing out of the drawers and onto the floor. When he came to the bedside table and hit the bottom drawer he stood erect, quietly staring inside.

    Previously, I'd placed the framed photo with the faces showing, so that I could torture myself with the occasional gaze upon the smiling couple. My head hoped that Drake had found his happiness again in the arms of his first love but my heart rejected the glee. Pangs of jealousy always caused me to slam close the drawer and swear never to succumb to the temptation again. Still, I'd never packed it away for the same reason I'd never boxed Drake's clothes. The *what if's* always gave me a false sense of hope.

    I watched the young Indian as he bent again and pulled the picture to within inches of his face. His concentration heightened and I wondered if now would be the time to run. But, it was already too late. I was hooked. I watched his array of expressions and grew mesmerized with the notions competing inside my head. While at the same time, my heart understood that something deeper transpired before my eyes.

    I inched closer and pulled the drawing from the same drawer. I passed it to him and he startled, as if surprised I was still in the same room. So was I. But, I put on a brave front as he snatched the paper from my hands. When confusion betrayed him, I pointed to him and said, "you." He debated something on the inside and turned to leave, pictures in tow. This would never do.

    "Drake? Is your father alright?" I asked.

    His muscles tightened and I saw anger emerge from a dark place within. Without another word he grabbed a blanket off the bed, threw it at me, and pushed me into the kitchen toward the door. He undid the latch and heaved me outside.

How did he get in? Maybe, when I went outside – hopefully the last time, after the bath, and not the time before to get the tub. Remembering how nervous I'd felt the entire time I bathed, I shuddered and wrapped the blanket tighter around my shoulders.

Chapter 11

We'd rode hard and I found my head swaying, dizzy in the early morning sun and from lack of food. I wrapped the blanket securely under me to keep it from falling off. When I could keep the pace no longer, I tapped the Indian on the shoulder. He pulled hard on the reins and turned to face me.

"I'm hungry and tired. Can we stop?" I began to doubt that he understood much English, or perhaps it was simply selective listening on his part. He'd only responded to a few chosen phrases since the abduction and usually with a grunt. This last request he appeared to understand for he proceeded to swing his leg over the side and pull me down, rather unceremoniously, after him.

"Sit!" he said pointing to a rock. He withdrew a small pouch and out came long strands of dried meat. Jerky – definitely not my favorite, but it appeared it was all he carried with him on the trip to the ranch. "Eat!"

Obediently, I choked the food down and then drank water from the flask he offered. It would suffice. In all my days it had never entered my mind that I'd be found riding the trails with an

Indian. I could only hope that he was Drake's son and that he was taking me to the man who would not see any harm come to me – of course, that was only relevant if Drake had any influence of persuasion with the tribe he now lived with.

Once seated behind the Indian on the horse again, I tried to focus on the scenery. The untouched nature had a wild beauty that captivated me and its scent helped to overcome the oily sweaty stench coming from the shirtless rider directly in front of me. He was obviously not chilled on this cool September morning, for in a weak moment earlier, when I'd offered to share my blanket, he'd grunted his disapproval with a scornful turn of the lips that reminded me of my position and caused me to say no more to the man. It appeared the less communication on this trek, the better.

At strategic points throughout the day, like breakfast, lunch and supper, I imagined that the troops had gathered together and were riding full tilt toward us with the sole purpose of rescuing me. Silently, I feared this young man's actions would break the peace that had survived many years in these parts. I did not want to be the cause of another uprising between the two peoples and couldn't bear shouldering responsibility for the bloodshed to follow.

Then I began to notice strange things the Indian did. Like brushing the hoof tracks, going in circles, breaking twigs on paths we didn't follow, riding on rock and through streams. I wondered if all his backtracking and side maneuvers added additional hours to the day. Perhaps we were not so far from Aspen Glen as it appeared. I was lost and had no way of knowing for sure.

It was early the second morning when I caught sight of the village. It covered a vast area of flat land, a river wound around its feet, and a breathtaking mountain range posed in the background. A sea of tents spread before me, and the crossed poles that reached to the sky were draped with leather hides. Women dressed in tunics, busied themselves close by, and the aroma that filled the air from their cook fires smelled strong of wild herbs.

    Men seemed to be out of the picture until all at once they surrounded us. Involuntarily, I clung to the Indian whom I traveled with and listened as the others laughed and mocked us. He threw me to the ground carelessly, jumped down and bound my wrists with a long piece of rope. He mounted his painted pony again and led me into the camp, my feet stumbling to keep up to the steady pace of the horses. The conqueror was bringing his prisoner home for all to see and his victim was drenched in fear and uncertainty. My future with this tribe did not look good, and suddenly I dreaded that the journey of the last two days had ended.

    When we stopped in front of a big central tent my captor pushed me forward and I fell to my knees. My clean white nightgown with a delicately embroidered collar now reeked of sweat and was spattered with dirt and blood. I had no idea the state of my face or my hair. What did it matter? The less appealing, the better.

    When the mockers silenced, I chanced to glance up. Directly in front of me stood an undersized older man wearing an oversized headdress made with layers of colorful feathers. I noticed his solemn expression and it quieted any defiance left in me. The young brave beside him made up for his chief's lack of showmanship, and spit on the ground next to me. The assistant – I assumed – barked strange words to the young man who had brought me into the camp. In turn, my abductor's verbal response to the one that spouted anger in our faces was riddled in a threatening, quarrelsome tone.

    All quieted when the Chief lifted his arm.

    The conversation from then on sounded respectful to the

ear but angry and heated in nature. My captor dragged me to my feet. "Mine!"

The Chief slowly nodded yes, and I became the property of Drake's son - hopefully. I still clung to the whim that the ranch cook was here somewhere and would ride in and rescue his maiden.

I listened as the chief spoke in broken English, addressing the angry brave who stood beside him and who appeared to be of some tribal importance. "It's too late!" Then to my abductor, "You should not have brought her here. The blood of many will be on your hands."

A voice from behind spoke up strong and challenging. I immediately recognized his intonation but not his tongue. Drake spoke in foreign words, while totally ignoring me and never once casting a sideways glance in my direction. When the confrontation was over the mob came and carried me to a nearby tree. They used the rope to bind me and wandered off – leaving me alone to imagine all sorts of possible scenarios. Shortly after, Drake appeared in front of me.

I gasped. "You're so quiet and sneaky – like them. You startled me."

He ignored that accusation. "I'm sorry that Drifting Wind brought you here. He disappeared days ago and I've been on edge wondering what he was up to," Drake said. Still he kept his distance from me, glancing behind him at intervals and staring hard at the young Indian that hovered close by.

Drake's glare managed to keep the brave at bay, or so I surmised by their silent scrutiny of one another. It was all so strange. I felt like a cat thrown into a stream – scrambling to escape – but held captive by the currents.

"I've bargained for ya, and in doin' so have offended the proud man. He apparently figures he can get his revenge by ownin' my woman and havin' his way with ya."

"Your woman? Why would he assume that?" I asked.

"He said that he found you in my bed. In his eyes, that settled the matter."

I blushed but realized now was not the time or place to tell him I'd replaced him in the kitchen at the Jones Star Ranch. Those facts were insignificant to our survival in this Indian camp.

"For heaven's sake," I said. "I'm old enough to be the boy's mother. The whole idea is absurd. Besides, why would he want to get his revenge with you? What have you done?"

"Nothing – and everything. He's lived a hard life, snubbed by family, and raised under the influence of jealous braves. His peers mock and use him. He falsely thinks his latest conquest will clinch his rights for acceptance with the tribe."

I started to interrupt, but Drake shut me down.

"Clare, we have little time. I need to stop this threat of an uprisin' between our peoples and keep ya safe at the same time. I need ya to trust me."

"I trust you, Drake."

"Good. I'm goin' to prepare for the tribal challenge to win you. Pray hard that I do, Clare, for both our sakes. Your captor is young and in all likelihood strong enough to hammer me to a pulp."

"Is this a life and death challenge and are you prepared to kill your own son?" His face portrayed nothing. "He is your son, is he not, Drake?"

"My flesh and blood, yes, but not my son any longer. His anger rules his heart and his lifelong obsession of tryin' to fit in here with his mother's tribe has made him bitter." Dark shadows of regret covered Drake's face. "And to answer your other question – no, this is not a life and death battle. This is a test of fitness, and I fear I have eaten too many sweet treats and lack the muscle it will take to win."

"I shall pray that the Lord will use you in this test to bring about good results for us and for your son," I said.

"Thank you."

I watched as his shoulders slumped and he walked off into the distance. So many unanswered questions still tormented me, and if tomorrow did not go in Drake's favor, I might never have them answered. One ray of hope shone through. This was the band of Indians that the Sheriff had spied on when investigating Drake's disappearance. The cook from Jones Star Ranch was indeed here, just as the lawman had claimed. Surely the rescuers would look here in this village. I leaned against the back of the tree, serious doubts troubling me. They'd look here only if someone were up in the middle of the night to see me ride away on the back of a horse with an Indian. What were the chances of that?

A bowl of mush was brought to me for supper. A young woman fed me every spoonful while remaining silent the entire time, but her inquisitive stare and obvious contempt spoke volumes. She left, and I was thankful that I'd not choked from the oversized scoops that she'd forced into my mouth. A while later, she returned to the tree, untied me and let me relieve myself in a nearby bush. At the tree again, she tied the knots, tighter than Drifting Wind had done. She tossed the blanket I'd brought from home across my body and mumbled something that might be interrupted in English as *good night,* or *freeze to death for all I care*. From her tone, the latter choice was the safest guess.

It was a long night and I heard every cry of the wild, wondering when and if they'd pounce from behind and save father and son the fight for slavery rights. I tried to calm myself. Drake would take me safely home if he won but the young man had a score to settle and his torment will have just begun. Drake was not confident of his chances and after sizing up the two, he was probably right. I took my fears to the Lord. The stars were brilliant tonight and I knew PJ and Ruth Ellen would be petitioning God for my safe return. I joined with them and a peace fell on me like a warm mantle.

Daylight was breaking through when I heard the drums and chanting. Dancing this time of day was surely not the norm – anything I'd read concerning the redskins was that they danced under the stars and flickering firelight. But, I was definitely not an expert on native traditions. Perhaps this was a final appeal to their Great Spirit for guidance in the upcoming challenge.

I wiggled and stretched my stiff body, while scanning the area to see if Drake and his son had gathered with the crowd. The woman from yesterday came again and shoved more mush into my mouth until I pressed my lips together tightly and refused the next spoonful. She stood and left. A short while later the drums stopped and two young Indians approached the tree. One untied me and the other yanked me to my feet. I stumbled from my cramped position, and he began to drag me.

"Enough of this dragging." I pronounced it loud enough so that the language barrier would not lose the meaning in the translation. I mustered all the strength I could, wrenched my hand free from the unsuspecting brave, and pushed myself to a standing posture.

I tossed my head high in the air and walked between the two as they led me up a rocky hill to the south of where I'd been left to wait all night. If I were never to return to this place, I determined to show these people that white women, or any woman for that matter, possessed a force worthy of respect.

The tribe trudged behind, like mourners to a funeral. Still I saw no sight of the male competitors. At a low plateau we came to a halt, and out came the rope. There was a red painted stake – which I hoped wasn't blood – and I was tied to it. Soon Drake and Drifting Wind appeared, both bare chested wearing a breechcloth around their waist instead of leggings. I chilled at the sight for the morning was cool, but realized that the physical efforts soon to be exerted would warm their bodies. The Chief appeared on the rock ledge as a stately figure, and next to him, his wife wore a tunic fringed and decorated with beadwork and porcupine quills.

They faced the competitors and the rules of the challenge were outlined in native tongue and then again in broken English – I supposed for my benefit. My position at the stake was both the starting and finishing line. The natural landscape presented the racers with daring and life-threatening obstacles. The goal was to be the first one to make it back to my location where the winner's prize – me, the sought-after slave - waited, bound and helpless, destined to go home with him. What I hadn't realized was that if neither made it to my side by the time the sun was high in the sky I would be set free, and both men would be shamed and shunned. I glanced at Drake when my chance at freedom was thrown into the mix and saw his mind playing with options. The only way someone would not return was if they killed or maimed one another and that was not an option to my way of thinking. I attempted to relay the message to Drake with a grim expression. I'd not take freedom at someone else's expense.

Drake stood on one side of the stake and offered me a faint smile, and his son stood on the other grinning like a schoolboy too big for his britches. Hopefully Drake could use that attitude to his advantage. It might be the only one he had. In his hand, the Chief held a feather decorated spear and he lifted it high concentrating his gaze on the morning sky. As we all paused with baited breath, a silence that smelled of death filled the air.

When the sun touched the horizon, the Chief's arm dropped, and the men took off running. I watched father and son until they rounded the corner and sped out of view.

I let out a long and weary breath – then closed my eyes. My spirit had never stopped praying for the outcome of this event, but now my mind joined in. The trouble with human reasoning is that I began to think of possible solutions for the Lord. As if He needed my help. I became conscious of the fact that He saw the entire picture, from start to finish, not only of this race but also of our lives. In the end, I gave it over to Him and asked for the grace to walk His path no matter the outcome.

When I opened my eyes, most of the tribe had returned to camp. From my position, I could see them busy with their daily routines as if nothing of importance was occurring on this mountain where three people awaited their fate. The two men that had escorted me to where I now sat tied to the stake, stood in silence on each side of me like soldiers at a gatepost.

Seconds stretched to minutes. I slipped into a mind-doze where time stood still. When a cool breeze swept over my face, it startled me awake. How could I nod off at such an hour as this? I needed to stand in the gap for Drake. He must be exhausted. I concentrated on the memory of his face, willing with all my might that he should feel my support and my love. I glanced to the sky, squinting from the glare of the sun that crept upward toward noonday; my appointed freedom time, should the racers not return to claim me. As much as I yearned to go home, I wanted more to go home with Drake.

Prayer would not form sentences in my weary brain. The truth of God's amazing grace prevailed in my heart and from the depths of my spirit the hymn rose within me. I began to hum. When I noticed the Indians beside me peek my way, I decided to sing the words. I'd sing my man home and perhaps a couple of heathen souls as well. I closed out the world and the melody started, low at first, but as faith grew I bellowed it out and hoped the entire village and the two struggling men on the mountain would hear the words of life.

Shortly afterward, I felt the blinding sun hot on my face. Surely it was noon and our destiny was at hand. Drifting Wind stumbled round the corner. He was limping and his face showed signs of struggle and fatigue. A hand reached out from behind and pulled him down. I watched in horror as Drake looked to the clock in the sky and tackled his son. They both went down, arms flailing about, neither hitting their mark often or with much force to their punch. Bloody faces and torn skin hung from their legs and arms and I bled emotionally inside for the men – both of them I was surprised to admit.

The officials topped the plateau and they gazed on the scene of tumbling men deprived of energy to crawl another step toward the stake. The young warrior looked up and saw his Chief and drew strength in that moment. With renewed strength, he pushed Drake. I watched as his shattered body collapsed and I cringed when I heard his skull crack against the rock. Then he lay deathly still.

The Indian struggled forward, step by step, inching his way closer to me, all the while watching the blank expression pasted on the Chief's face. I wondered what he'd hoped to gain by agreeing to this challenge. If he'd never been accepted throughout his growing years, why would he think this victory would win him favor in the eyes of the village and the man who ruled it? What twisted sense of hurt blinded the young man to believe he had a prosperous future with these people?

As it turned out – the young Indian did win one thing – a future with me. He collapsed across my knees just as the sun shone fully upon us. My lips trembled and I lifted my eyes heavenward. Somehow in my defeat, I felt a victory welling up inside me. God wasn't finished with us yet.

Chapter 12

I heard a groan and then silence. Blood flowed back into my legs after the warriors hauled the unconscious body off me. They carried him down the hill and I continued to sit. Two more braves appeared and dragged Drake off as well. Still I sat. The Chief stared at me, and I wondered what was running through his head. He shouted an order and then he left. Two women came with a flask of drinking water and I drank it until one pulled it away shaking her head. I realized I was drinking too fast. I uttered a half-hearted thank you, and then felt the cold cloth sweep across my face. I leaned into it and enjoyed this touch of pampering. One squaw crept to the backside of the stake and began to untie me. When done she took the same cloth and massaged my wrists and hands. All the while she worked at regaining the blood flow she stared at me with round sober eyes. I managed a smile and saw the questions creep in behind her façade. Kindness – was that my mission, to show mercy to my captors? With God's help I would endeavor to be his hand extended.

The women helped me to my feet and braced me between them as we wobbled down the mountainside. By the time we reached the appointed tent I felt stronger and could stand on my own. One opened the flap and waited for me to go inside. It was dingy and stank of animal hides, but the assault on my nostrils took second place when I saw Drake and his son lying on mats on opposite sides of the tent. I hurried toward Drake but the girl held me back and pushed me toward the young man who'd won the challenge. When I continued to hesitate she pointed to the still body and urged me with stern, robust actions to go there first. I inched toward the man assuming that he would be my number one concern, but the fact that Drake had been brought into the same tent gave me hope that I would also be able to care for him.

I noticed a dented tin pan and picked it up. "Water?" I tried to communicate.

The one girl who remained with me grabbed my hand and pulled me outside. She hauled me down an incline and pointed to the river. I walked in with my bare feet and felt revived by the chill of the cool water. The girl was watching closely, so I bent to fill the pan. Almost immediately, her voice called out, and with a pointed finger beckoned for me to return to the camp. So much for selfish indulgence but I didn't mind. All I wanted was to get the young man cleaned up and tend to his father. With renewed vigor, I lunged ahead of her and raced back up the grassy slope. She caught up and together we went inside the tent.

She stood at the door and watched me bathe Drifting Wind. Her eyes lingered on him and I wondered if she were the only person in this village who actually cared for his well being, or was her participation simply an act of obedience. The soft green eyes that fell on the still form told me she was happy to be here with us in the tent.

Then it hit me – green eyes? Did Indians have green eyes?

I examined her closer and noticed her skin was lighter; in fact, the brown resembled a burnt-in tan. She was a white girl! Perhaps taken the same as I?

I attempted conversation. "Do you speak English?" I asked.

Her petite figure squirmed in fear as she glanced over her shoulder. No word uttered from her lips, but as I waited a slight nod up and down was offered. I was ecstatic. Somehow it felt good not to be the only white woman in the entire village. But she was afraid. I'd have to be careful – consider any consequences she may suffer by speaking with me. I decided to simply talk to myself and allow her to listen.

"I can see you're concerned about Drifting Wind. He appears to be in good condition." I felt around his body. "Possibly some cracked ribs and a broken leg. I'm not a nurse but I've seen doctors wrap the ribs tight to keep them from jostling about. Do you have a very long clean cloth that I can use?"

The girl disappeared from the tent and within minutes was back with thick strips of an old gingham dress. She passed it to me and backed off.

"The pattern is lovely. Did you wear it when you were younger?" She nodded and I continued. "Would you help me wrap Drifting Wind? You just need to sit on the other side and when the material comes out from behind his back you can cross it over his chest and pass it to me." When she hung back, I said, "It's easier with two people. I also want to make a splint for his leg and then see to his father's head wound as quickly as possible."

She moved into position and together we bound the young Indian. I watched her closely but could not read her feelings for Drake's son. Perhaps she cared, but to what degree I couldn't tell. She hid her feelings well, likely a well-learned survival tactic.

When done I created a splint which held his leg tight between the sticks. At least that would keep the young victor on his back for a while. Taking a light blanket, I covered his unconscious body.

"He'll remain asleep for a while. If you know of any herbal remedy for pain would you please gather it for him. When he wakes he will hurt." She jumped at the suggestion and hurried back outside.

I grabbed the opportunity and quickly moved in beside Drake. I knelt and touched his bloody hand while a tear trickled down my cheek. Leaning my head against his chest I heard a steady heartbeat. Thank God. I noted the need for fresh water but at the same time did not want to miss this time with him. His recovery won the debate. Infection would never heal without the doctor's medicine, yet perhaps the girl knew of a natural one to help Drake – if she cared.

I hurried with the pan to the river again. This time I bent and scooped the cool liquid in quickly and started back towards the village. Out of the corner of my eye I noticed a young brave watching me – probably he'd been assigned to keep me from wandering too far from my tent. I chuckled. Where would I go? I had no idea where on God's green earth I was and what direction to take to run home.

Drake was my best chance to make it out of here alive, and I desired more than anything that he would stand strong and walk out with me. Often concussions were serious and could be life threatening. I knew nothing of the workings inside a person's head. Ruth Ellen had barely escaped her accident in Aspen Glen – managing to come out with a memory loss that had caused PJ great grief. Would the same thing happen to Drake? Would he forget he ever knew me? Our time together had been so short – but meaningful. It had not taken me long to fall in love, once the right man entered my life.

Inside the tent I bathed Drake from head to toe. I took some leftover cloth strips and started to wrap the gaping cut on his head. A hand stopped me. The girl held out an herbal mixture and nodded to Drake's head. Gratefulness flooded me – for nature's medicine and for the kindness she'd shown me in preparing it. While I dabbed his injury with the paste, and then smeared the cloth with the goo, I watched the girl mix another wooden bowl of ingredients, and when done she placed it by Drifting Wind's silent form. Painkiller.

"Will you show me how to mix these medicines? God's nature provides so many healthy ingredients that I don't how to use."

She nodded. Her stable expression broke and released the hint of a smile that curved her full lips upwards. She was beautiful and I hoped she would stay.

"Will you be allowed to remain here while I nurse these men back to health?" I asked.

This time she spoke. "I am here to interpret for you and teach you in the ways of being a good mate for Drifting Wind." She looked sideways at the young man on the mat and her smile faded. She did have feelings for Drake's son.

"Please, I will not make a good mate for your young man and I will do everything within my power to dissuade him. You, on the other hand, would be his perfect choice." I affirmed that for her benefit because I knew she'd resigned to living with this tribe the rest of her life and had chosen the Indian no one else cared about. Two outcasts would be a great comfort amongst a people who mocked their white blood.

"Not your choice," she said. "Drifting Wind will decide."

"He's never seen me in the morning," I laughed to ease the tension. "That should bring him to his senses real quick."

The girl managed a second smile and said no more. She sat on her knees so her face would be the first thing that Drifting

Wind saw when he awoke. It backfired. When his eyes did finally open in the shadows of the fading sun, he sat upright and squealed, surprised by the pain. When she fussed with him, he slapped her hard and she scurried to the back of the tent like a whipped puppy. I forced myself to my feet, stretching to get the blood circulating again. I moved in his direction. I realized he was my responsibility, and that he expected me to serve him.

He watched me in silence. I picked up the bowl of painkiller and realized I had no idea how to administer it. I'd better start our relationship off on the right foot and reactivate the self-confidence that lay hidden in the pit of my stomach.

"Drifting Wind," I began. "I would not be so quick to shun this young woman and her potions. I understand these herbs will help you not squeal in agony like a little girl." Perhaps that was taking my authority a bit too far, but I never backed down even when I saw a trace of anger. I held his stare and then smiled – a fake one – but he had no way of knowing that. "Now be a good patient and take your medicine." I called out to the girl cowering in the corner. "Come now, it's okay. I will watch how you do it the first time so you need never become his punching bag again."

She inched forward and drenched me with unasked questions. I figured one might be – where did a woman your age get such nerve? And if I were to answer that I might say it is the very fact that I am a woman of this age. I hoped that the middle-aged members of this community were respected to some degree. It didn't matter. I resolved that I, as the newest one in their midst, would be respected, or I'd gladly take my leave of this world and take up residence in my eternal home.

Drifting Wind barked an order and the girl jumped. She administered the herb and helped him fall back against the roll of soft animal skins he used for a pillow. I thought I saw him mellow, ever so slightly. The girl obviously did, for she was smiling when she glanced up again.

"He will sleep now." She resumed her position at the head of his mat and sat cross-legged to wait.

"Perhaps you should lie down as well and rest. Night is coming soon."

Instead, she jumped to her feet and disappeared outside. Ten minutes later she returned with two bowls and cornbread. This time I could see chunks of meat and a few wild vegetables, turnip, beans and spinach, floating in a thick brown liquid swimming with specks of roots and herbs. I could handle this meal. In fact, I was starved.

"Thank you. What's your name?"

We sat on a mat close to the door to catch the last remaining light of the day. "They call me Whipping Girl because they use me to ward off the angry spirits, and provide a moving target for braves to practice their aim with war hatchets and clubs."

I gasped. "Surely not!"

"My skin has grown tough, but I have hoped daily for the brave to come forward who will find a reason to marry me and end the sacrificial duty that has been mine alone to bear."

"And you were hoping Drifting Wind would be the one?" I asked.

"Impossible now. He brought you here, so I will not be considered for his mate."

"I told you before, I will discourage the man. I have no intention of *mating* with him. I am past the years of childbearing and cannot provide him what he needs – a family."

"You talk brave, but when he recovers, you will bow to his roar. The tribal men have no use for him because he is a half-breed, so he takes his anger out on any woman who dares to cross his path."

"What of his mother?"

"When I arrived I was told she was dead."

A voice close by interrupted. "Why don't ya ask me that question, Clare?"

I placed my bowl off to the side and hurried toward Drake. Falling to my knees I hugged him fiercely before I remembering his injuries. I pushed back and blushed. "Sorry! But Drake, I am thrilled to hear your voice. You had a nasty blow to the head and I was afraid…"

He filled in the blank. "That I'd forget this whole rotten experience. No such luck. I recall very well my helpless position to aid you after you arrived in the village. But, mostly I recall all the agony my son has put you through with this ridiculous challenge! I will never forgive him for bringin' ya here."

"Oh, no, Drake. God has forgiven much. Who are we to hold bitterness in our hearts for our fellow man?"

"Ya can still be gracious, even after today?"

"Especially after today. Drifting Wind has answered my heart's prayer. When I thought you were dead to me, God has now shown me otherwise. You left so suddenly, and I lost all hope of ever seeing you again."

"And seein' me now, in this place, makes ya happy? Yer a strange woman, Clare Jones."

I laughed impulsively, for it felt so right to be anywhere with Drake again." Yes – I feel oddly high. Like someone has given me a shot of that whiskey you men seem to devour like water."

"Ya sound like you've been drinkin' a fair share too." Then he smiled and his face lit up with all the good things that I recalled about the man. All was well in my heart again.

"So, about the woman who was your wife? Will you tell me her story?" I asked.

"I met her one-day in the woods. She was cryin' and carryin' on about hatin' her family. She was born for better things. You know, all that nonsense that young girls sputter who are born amongst the upper-class."

"She spoke to you in English?"

"Naw, I knew her language. Used to do some tradin' back in the day with the tribe. Well, after that first time she'd sneak out often, and for over a month we got acquainted. Her tears dried up. She was fun and full of life with me, but sadly suffocated by tribal traditions. She was Chief Kicking Stone's daughter and destined to tie the knot with some wild brave she detested."

"Liar!" came a voice out of the darkness on the other side of the tent. That would be the roar of the lion that Whipping Girl had warned me about. A loud thump and groan sent me running in his direction. He'd tried to stand up and discovered the splint I'd made for his broken leg. I hid the smile of relief that escaped my lips.

"Drifting Wind, you must lie still and recover. You have several broken ribs and your injured leg needs to heal." When his black eyes filled with new anger, I turned to Drake. "Your son does understand English, does he not?"

"Of course he does. Lived with his Ma and me for eight years. He's as white on the inside as you and me, though he won't admit it."

Silent scorn drifted across the room and I decided it was not a good day to settle this family's neglected matters of the heart.

"Drifting Wind and Drake – both of you need to sleep. This has been an extraordinary day and your bodies need to recover. Tomorrow you can tear one another apart with your fiery tongues." I threw the woven cover back over the shocked Indian and said emphatically, "Sleep!" I left and walked to the other side.

His voice stopped me in my tracks. "I won yer woman fair and square. She's mine, you remember that, old man."

My steps never faltered as I made my way to Drake's side. I sat close by. I felt his hand reach for mine, and squeeze it tenderly. "We'll get out this mess, Clare. Somehow."

"The Good Lord knows where we are but I am not sure anyone at home does. Your son kidnapped me during the night."

"I gathered that, since yer still wearing your nightgown." His grin lightened the pain in his features but caused me embarrassment.

I looked down in dismay. "Oh, my, and a very dirty nightgown, to be sure. I didn't have time to pack." My eyes sparked with amusement, and for a long moment I remained lost in his gaze.

I felt a hand on my shoulder. "In the morning I will bring you clothes and the white man's soap that I save for special occasions. You can bathe in the river and I will watch that no harm comes to you." I wondered what influence the captive white girl possessed over these people that would guarantee my safety.

Drake answered my unasked question. "You are her charge and the warriors will listen when she defends you." He lifted his eyes to the girl who towered over us. "Thank you, Whipping Girl. Clare will enjoy a dip in the cool water."

His smile told me he was teasing and I bit my lip. This interaction was too normal to enjoy in this horrid setting.

"Meanwhile, we all best turn in. Not much to do here after dark unless you're feeling up to dancin' around the fire with the natives." Drake patted my hand. "See you when the sun comes up."

"If you need me, don't be afraid to wake me," I said to Drake.

From the other side of the room I heard grumbling and a faint, "I won't." Then came Drifting Wind's snore, loud and spluttered, and I grinned.

Whipping girl moved to the back corner and motioned for me to follow. I held up one finger and turned to Drake.

I spoke low. "I'll not go another day without you telling me why you left the ranch so suddenly, with none of your belongings and no word to anyone. We were all so worried."

"The boy came. I could see he was in trouble. Had an arrow broke off in his arm. I fixed him up then he turned on me and demanded I go back to the village to make good for my past mistakes. He said I owed it to him and I supposed he was right. I'd stolen the Chief's daughter from under the tribe's nose, married her and started a family. Her father was not pleased and used to come and taunt us at the little house in the hills where we tried to live our lives without the Indian or the white man. We just wanted to be left alone."

"Then came the day of the fire and you presumed your wife and son to be dead, when in truth they were stolen back by her family and brought here?" I asked.

"The braves left all the right signs for me to read. I had no idea they were alive until Jerome showed up at the ranch."

"Jerome sounds much better than Drifting Wind. I shall call him that from now on."

"He'll spit on you," Drake warned.

"So be it. I'll wash it off."

"Do ya think ya can beat my son? He's strong and hates me. Using you to pay me back for deserting him and his mother is his latest pleasure. He has had few in his life."

"The Lord is my strength, Drake, and no one can fight His love for long."

"When I'm off this mat we will plan our escape. I will not leave you living in this village for long."

"Be careful. You're alive and you better stay that way," I said as I bent low and kissed him gently on the lips.

He grabbed my hand. "What of the good Doctor, Mrs. Jones?"

I smiled. "The good doctor and I have decided that we do friends best. A marital union should never have been spoken between us."

"Now I'm happy, too. Ever think we're just plain crazy? This is not a place of happiness."

"Anywhere you are is my happy place. Good night, Drake. Sweet dreams."

I moved slowly to the back of the tent and crawled in, still dirty, but feeling the best I had in weeks. Love had a way of outshining the grimmest of circumstances. As I settled under the blanket, a quiet voice whispered in my ear. "My given name was Sandra. I'd be pleased to hear you call me that."

"Goodnight Sandra. I will lift your name to the heavens and we shall watch His miracle unfold together."

Chapter 13

Sandra was true to her word and roused me from sleep at the breaking of dawn. "Quiet," she said as she pulled my sleepy figure to a standing position. The young woman led me outside and down to the river. She handed me the soap, comb, soft cloth for drying, and I watched as she hung a faded dress over a low hanging limb.

"It was my mother's and I'd be happy to see you wear it. I could have brought you a deerskin tunic, but I don't want to believe you will be here long enough to blend in with the others. You should always outshine the darkness."

"Surely these people are not so lost in darkness that the God of Light cannot turn them around," I said.

"Haven't seen no light; except in your eyes. My Pa was killed right off when they attacked our wagon. The warriors brought Ma and me here and hid us from the traders until eventually even they stopped coming. Ma died two years later but I've been here many summers. I come and go as I please. They know I would be lost in the white man's world. The memories fade more every year, but since you came I'm recalling little things." Her tone became wistful. "My Ma's laughter was like a song in the wind. And the way my Pa could sweet talk a wild horse then be riding him across the open meadow in no time flat... well, it pleases me to think on these things."

"Of course it does. They are your parents." I thought of Drake's family. "It's the same way for Jerome," I laughed at her vacant expression and explained myself, "Drifting Wind has a white father and an Indian mother. These are the facts, and the sooner he faces it, the sooner we can all go home."

"Do you believe it will be that easy?" she asked.

"Did I say easy? Heavens no! A man can be as stubborn as the day is long. But all days come to an end and so will this time in our lives. I have it from the best authority."

"Who might that be?"

"Why, the Lord, of course. He commands our days and our nights and promises that after a night of troubles a new morning will rise, and everything will be as it should."

"That sounds so magical."

"Not magic. It's my dramatic twist on His written word. But, you watch and see –it will come to pass."

I believed it even stronger after putting voice to it, and thanked Him that His mercies were new every morning. God knew we were in need of mercy.

I stuck my toe in the water and pulled it back screeching from the cold. This had sounded like a good idea last night but surely Indians did not bathe in rivers all winter long. There had to be a better way to cleanse oneself. Next time I would try a sponge bath with water warmed from the fire. But I was a newcomer here and chose not to rock the boat on this issue. Far greater concerns were held in the balance. It was the fastest wash of my life. The soap smelled wonderful but my head tingled from the frosty glaze on my scalp. The entire experience gave *refreshing* a whole new meaning.

I raced onto the shoreline and hurried to a nearby bush where Sandra waited with the cloth. She wrapped the large piece around my body and rubbed me furiously. I felt the circulation return and reached for the clothes she'd laid out for me, even down to undergarments. After three days, it felt good to shed the nightgown and stand fully dressed. I hugged her hard, wanting her to feel my heart-felt appreciation soaring through me into her.

"You are welcome," she said in response to my affection. "I don't remember wearing pretty dresses. The tribe gave me deerskin dresses and leggings on my first day here, but after Ma died I buried one of her favorite outfits in my special place. No one bothers me there."

"You'll have to show me sometime." I dried my hair the best I could with the wet cloth and started to comb the tats through.

"I can do braids, if you'd like," Sandra offered.

"I've never worn my hair like yours – in long twists – even as a child." I laughed. "I have braided the lengths in circles on top of my head, but this is not the time to blend in. My only influence to this tribe is as a white woman. I will leave it draped down over my shoulders."

"Hurry now. Drifting wind will be wanting food."

"Oh, dear, food! Will you help me prepare it, Sandra?"

"Yes, I have the fire started already.

Drifting Wind growled when I passed him his food. Plunging two fingers in the bowl – he scooped the mush into his mouth while berry juice dripped from his mouth. He devoured it like he hadn't eaten in a week. I thought I'd try out the new name. He couldn't be in any more of a foul mood than yesterday.

"Jerome." That got his attention immediately. "Did your parents not teach you any table manners at all – especially when in the presence of ladies?"

He grunted again and turned his attention to sliding his fingers around the bowl to scrape the last of the gruel. I persisted with my line of questioning. "Need I repeat myself?"

He looked at me as if I were the enemy. "You're not my mother! You will be my woman."

"I am old enough to be your mother and I will not be your woman. You require younger blood, one to bear you children and carry on your name. You must choose among the unmarried in the tribe." He seemed taken aback by my boldness, so I plunged in. No sense quitting now. I was either dead or getting through his thick skull. It was hard to decipher which. "Whipping Girl – or Sandra I like to call her – is young, smart and very beautiful. She will make lovely babies."

He jerked his head to the side where Sandra stood watching. She shrank from his glare and I'm certain if there had been a rabbit hole close by, she'd have jumped in and disappeared. But this time he did not roar in her face and I considered that to be a positive sign. Perhaps he'd been thinking of Sandra along these same lines, before he became distracted in settling the score with his father through me. That brought up more questions, and I pushed forward, common sense abandoning me.

"Why did you decide to look for your white father now, after all these years?" I could hear Drake clear his throat from behind. He probably thought I was treading into dangerous territory, but I stood taller and lifted my brows, letting the young man know I expected an answer. I felt elated when he offered one.

"The woman who bore me is gone fifteen summers and I need to take a mate. No woman will honor my name until I triumph over the man who betrayed me."

"And what makes you think your father betrayed you?" I asked.

"My grandfather said the white man stole her from the camp. He came one day to trade and then left. The Chief's girl child never returned from picking herbs that day and my grandmother wailed all night over the loss."

"Why do you suppose the Chief did not order his braves to chase them down and bring her back?" I asked.

"He did. When the braves finally found them, I'd been born and his daughter begged to stay with me at the cabin with the white man."

"That should prove to you that she loved your father," I said.

"Proves she was stupid, like all women," Jerome said with disgust in his voice.

"You don't believe that. You're upset that the tribesmen will not accept you and have turned bitter, first against your mother and now your father. When will the hate stop, Jerome?" I asked.

He hissed at me and made a swing but I shuffled my feet backward and his swat missed my legs. Unable to move with his leg holding him on the mat he yelled, "Get these sticks off my leg!"

"If I do that you will be a cripple. Time will heal it and then you can run, fish and hunt with your buddies here in the camp." I played with my speech until the words sounded like a mockery. He had no friends in this camp and both of us knew it.

Sandra ventured timidly into the conversation. "What did our Chief say was the reason you and your mother came to be at the village without your white father?"

I could see the wheels turning in Jerome's head, wondering whether the stolen white girl deserved to know of his past. In the end he gave into the plea behind her concerned eyes.

"Said at first he left us at the cabin to rot, but others snuck away to make trouble, especially her brother, Blazing Fire. Chief

Kicking Stone does not want to do anything to rile the white man and cause the fighting to start up again. So one day the Chief ordered they bring us home to the tribe and not make her husband suspicious. My father never came to look for us. Grandfather was happy, my mother cried, but I was angry. I never understood how any man could abandon us to these people who treated us like dirt."

Drake choked the words. "I am so sorry, Jerome. I loved you then and I love you now."

Jerome appeared surprised and confused. He peered at the man on the other side of the tent. Obviously the abandoned boy had never questioned his grandfather's rendition of his daughter's choice of husband. He growled. I was getting under his skin and considered letting him chew over the conversation thus far, but a voice prompting me from the inside failed to drop it. I hoped it was the Lord and not my stubbornness.

"Your father tells me of a wonderful life with a woman he loved and a boy he doted over. What did you do with the picture you snatched from the room when you kidnapped me?"

Involuntarily, he glanced toward his satchel lying close by. I went and brought it over and passed it to him. "Look at it again."

He fumbled with the flap and withdrew the wrinkled sheet of paper. He did as I asked. Lines of concentration etched across his forehead and no one in the tent spoke.

"I recall the game with the ball. I played it with... him." The word *him* stretched out between clenched teeth.

"Yes, you did. And your father was the proudest of men. Told me his son had a strong arm and could throw the ball clear across the river." Those were not Drake's exact words, but probably the Indian would not understand the length of a county. The river he could see outside his tent door.

"My father speaks of me?"

"Certainly! He loves you. But, his broken heart believed the lie the Indians left for him – that you'd both been burned in the cabin. Your father would never abandon his family. His heart has ached for many years."

The roar returned. "His aching heart is not good enough! I will steal his new woman and he will watch. Then he will know how deep a heart can break."

I started to speak but he put up his hand and threw the empty bowl at me. "Enough!" He fell back onto his bed.

I reached for the bowl of painkiller and administered it. Jerome settled down after that and soon filled the room with a gentle snore. I moved to the other side of the tent while Whipping Girl took her place at the head of Drifting Wood. I saw the devotion in her eyes and prayed these two would find love.

Drake was sitting up and smiling when I approached him. "You are full of surprises, aren't you, woman?"

"Ignorance of Indian customs help. I'm sure I am crossing the line of a captive slave but I don't care. Mending your torn past is all that matters, and Jerome has known much grief in his lifetime. God can heal both your hearts and give you a new beginning."

"With you being wife to us both?" I caught his teasing smile.

"Don't be silly. I will never marry your son. Sandra will take my place. You wait and see."

"You are right. You are ignorant in the ways of the Indian," he said.

"But not in the ways of the Lord and he will have the final say."

"I almost believe it when you say it."

"You should. Now let me get you a bowl of that breakfast mush and we'll sit and dream of smoked bacon, fried potatoes, and farm fresh eggs; all washed down with the black coffee and topped off with your famous cinnamon rolls."

"Stop it right now. I miss my kitchen more than you can guess."

"I've been keeping it for you." I backtracked. "That's not entirely true. In the beginning when I felt sure you'd return any day, I fed your cowboys and kept your kitchen clean. PJ sent the Sheriff looking for you and he found you, here, walking around like you owned the place." I laughed. "I can see now how one can walk freely and still be a prisoner. I'm sorry he didn't come into the camp and rescue you that day, but he assured us you were here of your own free will and he'd not risk an uprising with the Indians."

"Smart man," Drake said.

"When he returned, and I'd found the picture of your family in the bottom drawer, I surmised that news had come that your wife and boy were alive and you'd run to them – as you should. My heart grieved but I rallied myself free of its grip and felt truly happy that your past was finally at peace."

"Yeah, you can see the faulty thinkin' there, right?"

"Not for me. For here you are, sitting before me in the flesh, and all I can do is thank God for a second chance. I love you, Drake Whitfield, and I'll not be apologizing for that anymore."

"I never wanted you to. You already know that I love you. I spit it out like a jealous schoolboy at the picnic and left you to think it over, never dreaming all this would take place the next week."

"There's more. When I settled in my mind you were not going to return, I asked PJ to hire me for your job."

"What?"

"Yes, I actually get paid to feed your Cowboys and that night your son appeared was the first night in my new home. I moved in. What do you think of that?"

"Well, I'm thinkin' that when all this is over it will make the transition of bringin' my new wife to live with me back of the kitchen, much easier." He scratched his head. "Why ever would you wanna sleep in that dingy room when yer son has welcomed you into his grand home?"

"Because I'm breathing your air and touching your things. That was my comfort and I'd not allow anyone to take it from me. I had to beg PJ but finally he secured the building and let me stay. First night, I was kidnapped. He will blame himself for giving in. He has no idea where to look for me."

"If I know PJ, he'll never stop lookin' until he finds you."

"You're right there, and I'm banking on his stubbornness. I do not plan on living with Indians the rest of my life."

My face lit up and he smiled.

"So optimistic."

"You would be too if you could see my new space – our new space. I hired Jake to build an addition to your dingy room. I have a new bedroom, a small sewing room and a toilet in the woodshed. You will love it." I frowned. "Except it's not quite complete. Francine and Agnes were coming to help with the final touches. Oh, my, they will be so worried."

"They're mighty fine friends and will surely be prayin' up a storm." Drake shifted and pulled me into his arms. "Wonderin' if there be enough room fer two in that new bed of yers at the ranch?" He was quick to add, "Fer a husband, of course. Clare Jones, I was a fool not to pursue you. And to think the Doc got to proposin' first." He shook his head, and I lifted mine to gaze into his steamy eyes.

"Kiss me, Drake Whitfield, before the bear awakens and rips you to pieces for touching his woman."

His mouth smothered my laugh and I sunk into a place of safety, wishing this stolen moment would never end. When we came up for air, he whispered in my ear. "I gather that's a yes to my proposal?"

"It is a definite yes."

The flap of the tent pulled aside and light streaked across the floor of the tent and spotlighted Drake and me. Chief Kicking Stone stood there, silent and somber.

I jumped to my feet about the same time Sandra did. The Chief would not find favor with both of us sitting by the wrong men – not after declaring Drifting wind the winner of the challenge. He surveyed the scene and barked an order to the Indians by his side. They rushed in and grabbed Drake and began to drag him away.

"No please!" I cried but no one was listening.

The two returned and dragged Sandra from the tent as well. She glanced back at me and I saw the horror in her eyes. When everyone was gone the Chief pointed to the groggy Indian on the mat and said, "your man!" then let the flap close and left us alone.

The air tightened around me and I allowed tears to escape. I dropped to the floor and sobbed quietly until my stomach ached from holding the noise in. When I straightened and glanced toward Jerome he stared openly, but whatever he was thinking was masked.

"My father and Whipping Girl are gone?" It was a question he obviously knew the answer to.

"The Chief ordered them away." A thought came to me. "Drifting Wind, can you find out what has become of them? The braves were so rough and I fear for their lives."

A long minute stretched between us before he yelled in a loud voice for the guard to hear. The Indian I'd seen hanging around popped his head inside. They conversed in their native language and the guard departed.

"Thank you." I assumed he had done my request.

"I answered you because you addressed me as Drifting Wind. That is my name and I will only answer to it."

"I do prefer Jerome, because I believe deep down that is the person you are meant to be, but I will honor your request for now, Drifting Wind." Our talk was progressing well so I continued. "Why did the tribe name you that?"

"Cause I'd been drifting in the wind for eight long years before they brought me here. I felt pride at first but then discovered it was a front. Truth is, I'll be drifting the rest of my life with these people. It was never meant as a welcome home name but a label that would separate me from my mother's people. I am a laughing stock, even after I won you and disgraced my white father in their eyes. I cannot cross the chasm that my parents created with this people."

"Perhaps you should consider coming home with us. Drake lives and works on my son's ranch and I even have a room for you." The sewing room disappeared from my plan and instead I saw Drake's son in there with the old cot and furniture I'd painstakingly considered discarding. Another thought occurred to me. "Or better still, we could bring Whipping Girl with us and we can build you a cabin in the woods by the river. It's close by so we can visit whenever you like."

He listened. That's all I could hope for. The seed had been planted and I hoped that it would crack through his hardened heart and sprout new life for all of us.

A noisy commotion could be heard outside and I went to the flap to peer out. I gasped and was immediately pushed aside, tumbling to the sidewall of the tent. The guard had returned and now shouted something in his native tongue to Jerome. I saw the fear in the young man's face and I knew there was trouble brewing.

Chapter 14

While cowering in the corner, I watched Jerome's attempts to put weight on his broken leg. The whole camp was in uproar and the glimpse I'd seen outside the tent caused my heart to shrink in terror.

Jerome yelled at me and managed to stir me from my numbness. "Woman! Help me to stand." I rushed to his side just as he nearly toppled to the floor.

It sounded like a native-curse-word that spewed from his mouth before he muttered, "Get us outside. Now!" he ordered when I stared at him through blank eyes.

"How can we help your father and Sandra?" I asked.

"Go!" was his response. I stood on his injured side and wrapped his arm around my shoulder. "Lean on me when you need to. Otherwise, hop. You are a big man and I can hardly carry your full weight."

His hopping was awkward, but by the time we exited the tent and began our walk toward the gathering crowd, we'd developed a rhythm to our steps. The crowd parted as they saw us, and in the distance, I caught Drake's eye and held his gaze.

Time stood still, and the crowd silenced. The nearer we drew to him I observed Drake's expression changing as if coming back from the dead and into the light we shared.

It was then I noticed the pile of branches stacked around the stakes he and Sandra were tied to. They were to be burned alive! I peered toward Jerome and noted he too had seen the predicament the others were in. His eyes remained focused and when I turned back to Drake I saw that father and son were locked together in some private place. Sandra also looked on Drifting Wind and her eyes pleaded openly for mercy. Could Jerome grant mercy here? Did all our fates rest on this unpredictable man who dwelt in disillusionment and anger? I lifted a prayer.

Just then the Cavalry arrived. I'd read of such close calls with death in our country's history, but now to be numbered among them, was an eye-opener I did not wish to experience again - ever. A new blend of chaos was developing as the Sherriff, Patrick, Gerald, Daniel, Stanley and a whole posse of men rode into camp with a white flag flying high. Would the Indians honor peace in the midst of this anger that sifted through the air like rotten dung?

"We come in peace and seek a meeting with Chief Kicking Stone," called the Sherriff to the screeching Indians that danced alongside. The Chief, who watched their entrance into his camp, lifted his spear high in the air and the noise ceased. The crowd gathered around the band of horses and led the group along the final stretch of land that separated us.

I caught Patrick's gaze and smiled trying to appear reassuring. He remained stern and focused, alert and anticipating the unexpected. My son, such a frontiersman – I was so proud as he rode toward me.

The Sherriff dismounted and walked toward the Chief. They stood eye to eye before the lawman spoke.

"Chief Kicking Stone. Glad to see you are in good health." The leader of the clan did not reply, but listened. "You know this here action of late defies our agreement. Surely the Indian nation does not want more bloodshed. You remember the wars between our peoples not so long ago?"

"I remember and do not wish more of the same."

"Then why was this woman," he pointed toward me, "kidnapped from her home and brought here?"

"My grandson, Drifting Wind, spoke need for personal revenge. I felt inclined to honor. As you can see, no harm has come to the woman."

"But what of these others?" the Sherriff pointed to the ground where the captors sat tied to a stake in preparation to be burned to death. "You plan on killing this white man and… is that a white woman seated beside him?"

I was pleased that he'd seen through the native garb and spotted the natural paleness beneath the summer tan. Now Sandra would become part of the bargain for freedom.

"They dishonored our customs, and my grandson," the Chief said.

It was then Jerome entered the conversation and he directed his question to his grandfather. "Since when did you care about my honor?"

"I honor your mother's memory, not you."

"So why did you bring me here so long ago?"

"Your mother would not come without you. She would rather stay and die in the fire."

"And when instead she died in this place, from a broken heart…" Drifting Wind began but was silenced.

The Chief interrupted, displaying no feelings for the man before him. "When she died you became an orphan for the tribe to treat as they wished. The white in you is offensive."

"Why not cast me out, or return me to my white father?"

"You were of no concern to me. You chose to stay."

"I never knew I had a choice!" the young man yelled and the elders moved closer to defend their Chief.

I stepped forward. "This can all be settled quite easily…"

Blazing Fire stood beside the Chief. He was a full-blood son, the brother of Drake's wife, and Jerome's uncle. He took two full strides in my direction and backhanded me. I fell to the ground. "Silence woman!"

In the excitement of seeing an easy solution, I'd forgotten my status here as captive slave.

Patrick leapt off his horse and covered the distance between us in a heartbeat. He reached for my hand and helped me to my feet while daring the Indian who hit me to interfere.

"Relax, PJ. I'm fine. Not a good time for either of us to start a war."

I looked at the Sherriff for support. He tipped his hat to me – then addressed the Chief.

"This woman is respected as an important member of our community. So, here's the deal. Since you seem to not care about your grandson, I assume you also do not care about his father and the woman he brought here. You will release them into my hands and peace will continue among our people."

"Drifting Wind has been to me as a thorn from a porcupine. You can have him, his captive and his father." The Chief glanced toward Sandra and scowled. "You may as well take the other as well. Whipping girl is all that reminds my people that we have the white man for neighbors."

I exhaled, long and heavy. Thank you, Lord for Sandra.

My grateful heart swelled in hearing of her release as well. I supposed I'd always believed in my heart that my family would go free in the end, but to bring another lost soul out from slavery gave me an added reason to celebrate.

Patrick grabbed me into a bear hug that lasted a long

time. From over his shoulder I saw the ropes being cut from Drake and Sandra, and I managed a wink in his direction. I pulled away from my son and Drake flew in to replace him.

"Well, excuse me," said Patrick, with a pout, and then gave Drake a playful shove. "Pack your son's bags, Cook, and let's get out of here before anyone changes their mind."

I hurried to Sandra and scooped an arm through hers. "To your tent, Sandra. We are bringing you home."

"I have nothing of worth to bring out of here," she said. "You are wearing my mother's dress, the only thing I hold sacred."

"Well then, let's go and retrieve my dirty nightgown. I kind of like that one and I may need it on cold nights this winter."

Drake was passing by struggling with his hopping son, and muttered, "Cold? Not if I can help it."

I blushed and turned to Jerome. "You alright with how this all turned out? Are you willing to become my stepson and not my husband?" I smiled at that for I already knew the answer just by the way he looked at Sandra.

"I will gladly move to the side and let my old man bed you," Jerome said without so much as a bat of an eye.

"Bed me?" I blushed again at his simple description of married life. He'd learn soon enough that many factors held a man and woman together until death-do-us-part. I was counting on love – unconditional love.

We all went one last time to the tent, packed what little remained of a broken past, and went out to join the posse.

The accounts of our adventures were spun around the campfire that night. Our small group comprised of family, present and future, while the posse snuggled around another blaze telling Cowboy yarns of a different kind.

"So what do you think, Jerome? Will it be the sewing room or your own cabin nearby?" Drake asked then took a long slurp of his hot coffee.

"Maybe the sewing room while we build the cabin?" Jerome suggested.

Patrick spoke up. "Will you be looking for a job when your home is complete?"

"I'm not so dumb to believe your men will accept a half-breed so easily. Breaking into your world will be just as hard as living with my mother's family. It's the way of things."

"Folks like us have the power to change people's minds if we do it in love," I said.

"Drake – your woman is high on love," Jerome said.

Drake beamed and I blushed, still in wonder that a man possessed the ability to bring the flush to my face again.

Sandra moved closer to Jerome. "You will be welcome in my world, Drifting Wind, if you'll have me?"

"You will not address me with my Indian name any longer. That life is dead to us." I was never so pleased to hear those words.

"The same invitation is extended to the white boy, Jerome," Sandra said.

"I will consider your offer, but I do not wish to ruin the life of your children as my parents ruined mine."

"In our cabin in the woods we can be whoever we want to be and educate our children to be wise and forewarned."

I interrupted. "Do you have any family, other than your deceased parents, Sandra?"

"None that I am aware of, and none that matter in the future I choose with Jerome, if that's where your question is leading."

"No, just curious. They would be thrilled to know kin survived an Indian kidnapping," I said.

"As will yours," Sandra laughed. "What stories we will have to tell the children."

I glanced at Drake. "Yes, my grandchildren, if Drake doesn't back out of his proposal once he sees his new home at the ranch."

"Not likely, woman. I'll not let you out of my sight ever again," Drake said. "PJ, that Ma of yers is one hard customer. Those Indians didn't know what hit 'em after she showed up."

Jerome laughed. "Brave and smart, Father. You snagged yourself a great catch there. Best watch out or she'll soon be chief in your tent."

I lost him after *Father*. It seemed everyone else picked up on it as well. The group silenced and looked at Jerome. He realized what he'd said and shrugged his shoulders. "Practicing to see how it sounds. He is my father, right?"

"Right!" said Drake as he drew his son into his arms for a bear hug.

Tears gathered in the corners of my eyes. Patrick lifted his coffee cup into the air. "Cheers. We are all winners here tonight, with not one drop of bloodshed."

We all cheered and joined him in the toast. Jerome and Sandra appeared confused but slowly followed suit. In the future, they'd both need educated in many of the white man's customs.

"And until all our marriage vows are said, Sandra, you will be my guest at the homestead. If that's all right with you, PJ?"

"Moving back in already? I knew independence wouldn't last."

He laughed and held up his hands in mock surrender when he saw me about to object.

"Life changes when we least expect it," I said as I moved in next to Drake.

"Ruth Ellen will be pleased with some female company," said Patrick. The house is lonely without you, Ma."

"Don't get too comfy seein' her there, boss. Doesn't take

long for the preacher to say a few words and get the hitchin' done," Drake said.

"Boss? Did he call me boss, Ma? Didn't ya tell him he lost his job?"

I played along. "I might let him help me out in the mess hall from time to time. I make more money than he did, so he'd do well to stick to building cabins for a spell."

Drake appeared surprised. "Well, I'll be. Upshot by the boss's mother."

I bent close and planted a kiss on his lips. "No sir, upshot by your soon-to-be wife. That has a better ring to it."

Drake roared laughing. "And so begins the competition. PJ, did ya know yer Ma is as driven as a thoroughbred stomping out a prairie rattler?"

"Never quite heard it expressed like that, but it fits," Patrick said.

"PJ how far along is the renovation? I so wish I'd been able to finish it before Drake came home," I said, disappointed I could not give him a personal grand tour of our completed love nest.

"Well, you have your wish, Ma. Agnes and Francine have been at the ranch, beautifying your new abode since the last nail was pounded in. Painted and furnishings so grand that Cook will think he's moving into another world."

"I told you once before, Cook has a name and it's Drake – your soon-to-be step father. What do you think of that?"

"Lots of changes, that's what I think," said Patrick as he lifted his cup in the air again. "To growing the Jones family – all good and as it should be."

"Hear, hear." The cups rose again and the family was stamped as unified.

I grabbed Drake and Patrick by the hand, "Come with me boys," I said pulling them to a nearby clearing.

We stood under a canopy of stars and I motioned for them to look upward into the heavens. "PJ, I felt we should introduce my betrothed to the Jones custom."

"You're right, of course, and no better time than tonight – a night of answered prayer. You both realize it was a miracle you got out of that Indian village with your scalps in place, don't you?"

"I realize no such thing. I had it on good authority that God was in control," I said in no uncertain terms.

"And now we will give thanks," said Patrick, "as we do for all the blessings in our life, every night under the stars. Brings comfort to know no matter where a Jones may be found, we're all under the same canopy of love."

"I think I'm goin' to like being part of the Jones clan," said Drake as he squeezed my hand and we all gazed upward into our new destiny.

A star winked and blinked and I decided I'd name that one after Drake and the new vein of Jones blood about to be birthed through my union with this man and his half-breed son. Lives had been stricken with sickness, confusion, heartbreak, and near death, but not snuffed out, and we stood as a tribute to that victory. Changes were bound to come, and I prayed we'd be strong enough to conquer prejudices with the grace it would demand.

I hope you have enjoyed reading STRICKEN, by Marlene Bierworth, the fifth book in the Jones Star Series. Would you take a moment and return to store online where you purchased the book and leave a review?

Nothing complicated, just a few of your reactions, what you liked about the book, characters or story. Your review not only helps rankings online, but it will help other readers determine if this book is the right fit for them. Thank you for your help in this area.

If you haven't downloaded other books in this series find them all here:
https://www.amazon.com/author/marlenebierworth
along with other family titles from this author.

Here is the sign-up-form to receive a weekly romance Newsletter and Inspired thought.
http://eepurl.com/djNqjn
Or join in with other fans on Face Book here:
https://www.facebook.com/groups/1118008614903688
/

Turn the page for a short excerpt from AWAKEN: Book 6.

Excerpt from Chapter one of Awaken: Book 6

I wiped the last of the dust from my desk and grimaced at the dirt that had lodged under my perfectly manicured fingernails. Disgusting! I hated that I was responsible for the cleanliness of my schoolroom. Was it not enough that I had to maintain the small quarters inside the old church building that had been assigned to me as home? I sighed. This was a typical response, born from both from my mother's training and the reality that the pampering lifestyle of the young mistress of Lakeside Estate was a hard habit to break. It fed the coddled side of me, and I'd be remiss not to admit I dreaded the idea of fully breaking the comfy habit. Of course, even I realized that I could never pay for a maid on a teacher's salary. I doubt I could even buy a winter wardrobe. As of now, I'd be wearing last year's, outdated fashion. That should never be. I'd write Father. Surely he'd modify his rule of *no financial help from home* just this once. The price of new clothes was mere pocket change for him, and he'd not want his daughter walking about like a vagabond. My sigh came from a deeper spot within as I secretly wondered if I'd carried this yearning for independence a bit too far – whether this pioneering was worth all the bother.

I glanced at the rag in my hand. Mother would be appalled at the extent to which I'd fallen from society. The plan of her eldest daughter to enter the work force had been more than the privileged woman could handle. To think, at the nod of my head, I could be married to a wealthy man and be sipping tea with the board members that governed such professions as an educator. But, never in small town Montana! Heaven forbid! That was the final straw that had sent Mother to bed with a fierce headache, that continued to nag her up to, and including, the day I'd boarded the train to go West.

My mother cried and my father remained stone-faced as I'd waved goodbye from the window of the train – she distraught that she'd lost a daughter, and he confident I'd return before the year was out. I was elated to be going. I'd explored all the available adventures in my Boston spear of influence, even some not appropriate for the socialite, Miss Ferguson.

The Teacher's Academy I'd attended had daily pounded *the mission* into their students' minds – deliver information to the ignorant despite any opposition. Be firm and never back down. Yes, this was my classroom and the scatterbrained children I'd met thus far would need a firm hand indeed. A familiar feeling of power consumed me, and it reminded me again of home. I could do this! Control was one thing I'd been taught well. But, alas, the cleaning still bothered me. I threw the rag into the trashcan and then laughed aloud. The youngsters could probably care less, so why should I?

I straightened my form and felt the Ferguson stubbornness take its rightful place in my mind. This trip to the frontier need only be the experiment I'd first intended it to be. I'd follow this western adventure for as long as it suited my fancy and not one day longer.

My spirit rejuvenated as I scanned the one-room schoolhouse that Ruth Ellen's husband, Patrick Jones, had funded. Never before had a teacher stood at the front of this particular room, and if I were honest with myself, that had been a prime motivator in my decision to come. I felt exalted to be the first.

From a bag, I withdrew the shiny red apple that my father had purchased for me in a specialty store filled with exquisite souvenirs. It was his parting gift. With certain apprehensions, he appeared to understand my need for independence. According to him, modern women of worth were doing that these days. But I also knew he expected it to be a one year quest, and then I would return to sanity and move on with my appointed future in Boston. He'd reassured my mother with those exact words. The Ferguson clan were relieved that I'd traveled West in the company of the Joneses, who had once been born of the Thorncrest family – the latter name easing their apprehensions more than a mere Jones.

I had no idea where my future would take me, and that fact alone caused determination to stir within me. Liberation from the set-in-stone decrees of Boston society grew strength into my resolve and would keep me moving forward in search for that legendary pot of gold at the end of the rainbow. Not gold literally – for my family had no need for more of that – but gold of a different kind. Like the treasure that spilled from Ruth Ellen every time she entered a room. That's what I was here to discover, if the West possessed treasures worth my abandoning everything I'd ever known in Boston. I hoped a year was long enough.

In contrast, the jitters in my stomach caused me to doubt my surety in this new position. I stood as frightened as the children that would sit in chairs behind those brand new wooden desks tomorrow. It appeared we were all students of life, and both children and teacher had much to learn this school year. I hoped that might be the glue to bind us together as we explored the world of books and put feet to that knowledge.

Fresh air would end all this mind-muddle. Triumphant one minute and fearful the next was not my game plan. I stood tall and gazed out the back window, marveling at the way the breeze danced through the meadow filled with fall flowers. My feet felt the rhythm and produced a sudden urge to walk barefoot in the tall grasses. I wondered if Gerald would be free. I could always count on him dropping everything to do my bidding. My childhood friend, Ruth Ellen, with whom I'd stayed with for the first couple of weeks upon arrival, chided me constantly for such inconsideration. But I'm sure she'd agree that a single woman should not walk about the territory unescorted. This was, after all, the Wild West.

Hope you enjoyed the sneak peek at Book 6.
Will Chelan rise to the call to be a teacher in Montana before
she breaks the heart of every available bachelor in Aspen Glen?
Hope to see you in AWAKEN: To Tame A Teacher.

Made in the USA
Columbia, SC
19 December 2018